Bright Particular Star

By MARION GARTHWAITE

Cover by Marvin Friedman

SCHOLASTIC **SBS** BOOK SERVICES

Published by Scholastic Book Services, a division
of Scholastic Magazines, Inc., New York, N. Y.

The publisher is grateful to the following for permission to quote in chapter headings, lines from the following books:

From: "A Song of the English" from THE SEVEN SEAS by Rudyard Kipling. Copyright 1909 by Rudyard Kipling. Reprinted by permission of Mrs. George Bambridge and Doubleday and Co., Inc.
From: "Invictus" by William Ernest Henley. Reprinted by permission of Charles Scribner's Sons.
From: "Men and Women" by Robert Browning. Reprinted by permission of Houghton Mifflin Co.
From: "The Lesson" from THE FIVE NATIONS by Rudyard Kipling. Copyright 1903 by Rudyard Kipling. Reprinted by permission of Mrs. George Bambridge and Doubleday and Co., Inc.
From: HARVARD CLASSICS, Dr. Charles W. Eliot, editor. Reprinted by permission of P. F. Collier & Son Corporation.
From: "Crystal Moment" by Robert Coffin. Reprinted by permission of The Macmillan Co.
From: THE ART OF THE STORYTELLER by Marie Shedlock. Reprinted by permission of Dover Publications, Inc., New York, N. Y. 10010.
From: "Up-hill" by Christina G. Rossetti. Reprinted by permission of Little, Brown & Company.
From: "Love's Lantern" from JOYCE KILMER'S POEMS, ESSAYS AND LETTERS. Copyright 1914, 1917, 1918. Reprinted by permission of Doubleday and Co., Inc.
From: "The Children's Song" from PUCK OF POOK'S HILL by Rudyard Kipling. Copyright 1906 by Rudyard Kipling. Reprinted by permission of Mrs. George Bambridge and Doubleday and Co., Inc.

Single copy price 45¢.
Quantity prices available on request.

To MARIE HICKCOX

Because it is so hard to put into words
her years of kindness to me and mine

Thanks are due to the following librarians for reading this story in manuscript and for the benefit of
their constructive criticism:

Augusta Baker, Supervisor of Storytelling
New York Public Library

Jessie Boyd, Director of Public School Libraries
Oakland, California

Leone Garvey, Supervisor
Boys and Girls Department
Berkeley Public Library

Virginia Ross, County Librarian
San Mateo County Library

Betsy Schilpp, Children's Librarian
San Mateo County Library

Marian Trahan, Young People's Librarian
Oakland Public Library

and to

Lorraine Wallace, library page
for her teen-age evaluation

All the people in this story are fictitious. If the shoe happens to fit, I hope it doesn't pinch.

1

THROUGH THE WINDOW of the college classroom Torrey Thorne could look across the trees of the campus to the bay, across the water to the bridge that spanned the Golden Gate. It was a windless day in May, with Commencement just around the corner.

As the storyteller finished her tale, Torrey was thinking of ocean waves and a stretch of sand and . . . Cleve. When the class began the criticism of the story, Torrey leaned her head on her fist, absorbed in the secret game she had been playing ever since Cleve Macklin had slipped the diamond ring on her finger.

If she faced the ring toward the light and squinted down at it, she could see parts of the lecture room in the facets of the stone. She could see Dr. Jordan against the window. She could make out his flat head, with the long strands of hair combed carefully over his bald spot, the dark triangle of his Vandyke beard, and the broad shoulders Torrey was sure were padded inches beyond their normal span.

Torrey was still in a state of delighted shock over Cleve's proposal. She had known for two weeks that she loved him. She could see his gray eyes now, laughing down at her—was it just last Saturday? She could hear in her mind the waves plunging and roaring on the beach as the wind ruffled her dark hair and caught at the edges of the variegated beach towel that reached around the two of them, and Cleve slid the big diamond on her sandy finger.

"No job yet, Torrey," Cleve had said, "but I got word that I passed the Bar exams. That's all I've been waiting for. Say you love me the way I love you."

He hadn't waited for her answer as he took her face in his strong brown hands. He knew.

Torrey had looked down the beach over his shoulder to where Kate and Jeff were racing toward them, splashing through the shallow scallops of water and foam . . .

"Miss Thorne."

At the sound of Dr. Jordan's voice, Torrey came back to the class with a jolt. She slid the diamond around her finger hiding it in the palm of her hand. "I'm sorry, Dr. Jordan, I didn't catch the question."

Dr. Jordan removed his pince-nez, twirling the glasses at the end of the narrow black ribbon. His small, irritated eyes bored into Torrey's brown ones. "It was not a question, Miss Thorne. In case you're interested, I have been reading the names of those members of this class who have *not* completed the story assignments."

"I—" began Torrey.

"I have no record of a second story from you told to the children, Miss Thorne. And, as I understand it—pray correct me if I am mistaken—you still have a myth to present in class. I trust we shall be hearing these stories in the next few days?" There was rolling sarcasm in the question.

Torrey was appalled. How had she managed to get so far behind? Two stories on top of three finals, and that paper on Public Relations. It took her days to learn a story properly.

Dr. Jordan might be, in her opinion, a self-satisfied little pip-squeak, but he demanded and got from his class top quality in storytelling.

For the hundredth time since she had met Cleve, Torrey wondered why she had ever elected to take this course, along with the required work for her Library Science degree. She had told herself it was because she liked children and stories. But also it had sounded like relief from the heavy class work in cataloguing and reference. Dr. Jordan was a visiting instructor, pinch-hitting for the regular professor off on leave. She knew there had been a sneaking hope that it would be an easy way to pick up some needed credits.

Instead, this little man had run them all ragged with his demands. The first two months Torrey had enjoyed it. But that was before she had met Cleve.

Dr. Jordan turned back to the rest of the class. "We will devote these last few days to stories from the students on this list, to give them a chance to complete the required work." He teetered on his heels and flexed his knees in a conceited little bob.

Torrey's lip curled. Cleve would laugh when she

3

imitated the pompous little man, but it was sickening to have to sit and listen to him.

"I need not remind you," Dr. Jordan went on, with a threat behind his jovial manner, "that anyone not completing these assignments will be unable to get credit for this course." He looked straight at Torrey, his lips pursed.

Again Torrey felt a wave of panic. After the flu last semester she had dropped a course. Now she needed every credit to get her degree. Storytelling, she was thinking guiltily, was not the only course that had suffered this last semester.

When the buzzer sounded, Torrey's mind was churning. From the carefree joy of playing with the big diamond, of thinking of Cleve and the happy future they were planning together, she was plunged into too many things to do and too little time to get them done.

As she gathered up her books, she was thinking how foolish it would be to throw away the degree in Library Science she had worked all year to earn, and how unfair to her family. It hadn't been easy for Dad to finance this extra year. No matter how rosy her future looked as Mrs. Clevinger Macklin, she needed the added security of a degree behind her. It would be stupid, simply stupid, she was thinking, to lose it for two miserable stories.

"Just a minute, Miss Thorne." Dr. Jordan held up an imperative hand. He kept Torrey waiting at his desk while he handed out papers and answered questions. He finally gathered up his notes, sliding them into his soft pigskin brief case.

Torrey stood on one foot and then the other, fuming as she shifted her load of books. She wished she

I must warn you again. Your first work was top flight. If you can get the myth for class and the story for the children behind you, I might overlook the poor paper you handed in last week, and your inattention of the last few days. If not—" He left the threat hanging in mid-air. "Good morning."

As Torrey watched him leave the room she caught a glimpse of one of his students outside the door. "Oh, Dr. Jordan," purred Henrietta Mert's throbbing voice. "Just one more question. Isn't that Albanian story we heard today the same basic story as 'The Three Princesses of Connaught'?"

Henrietta Mert, Torrey was thinking, knew on which side her bread was buttered. Henrietta would never get two stories behind by the last week of Library School. She would always find the right questions to ask Dr. Jordan. But, thought Torrey, a person like Henrietta Mert would never, in all her born days, have any one in her life like Cleve Macklin.

With her heart singing, Torrey put her worries behind her and hurried out of the building to meet Cleve.

2

WHEN CLEVE WASN'T OUTSIDE, Torrey sat down on the stone steps in the sunshine to wait for him. She opened her notebook with determination to leaf through Dr. Jordan's lists of "Myths for Telling" to find one with which she was already familiar. But as the sunshine warmed her, she thought about Cleve instead.

How in the world, she thought, had a girl like Torrey Thorne been able to attract anybody as dear as Cleve? She'd known many boys and had liked some of them a lot, but not like this. It bothered her that she had known Cleve Macklin so short a time. Six weeks ago she had first met him. In little over a month they had fallen in love and were engaged to be married.

It frightened Torrey. Being married was forever. She belonged to the kind of family that took an engagement seriously, as a pledge. In the Thorne family you didn't accept an engagement ring without due consideration. Torrey was uncomfortably aware that this consideration was expected by the two families. Without consulting either family she and Cleve had agreed to an engagement. Cleve had sealed it with this outsized diamond that had been his mother's ring.

Torrey was sure her own family would like Cleve the minute they met him and had a chance to learn how dear he was. They would approve of Cleve— but not of the hasty engagement. She was sure that Mom and Dad would feel that way. Dave might back her up. Dave thought anything Torrey did was all right.

The thought of Cleve's family was even worse. Would they mind if he had taken the family ring from a safe-deposit box and given it to a strange girl they had never seen? Torrey was afraid they might.

Cleve hadn't talked much about his family. Torrey knew that his parents had been dead for many years. She gathered that the real head of the family was his godmother, who had raised him since his own mother's death. Cleve called her "Gang," but Torrey knew that she was Miss Cluney Mary Clevinger, who lived in the strange old house down the Peninsula. Torrey sensed that Cleve was a little afraid of her, and she felt sure that Gang was someone with whom she herself would have to reckon. She wished he had asked Miss Cluney Mary before he had taken the ring from the bank. She wished that she had met Miss Cluney Mary before she had accepted the ring. She wished . . . .

Then she saw Cleve striding down the path through the trees. Her heart did a quick turn, and she felt her face flushing. How lithe he was, his blond head set on broad shoulders, his gray eyes sparkling at the sight of her.

In the warm glow that wrapped around her at the sight of him she was sure this must be the real thing. All the little love affairs of high school and college had receded into their proper perspective. Nothing, no one but Cleve, mattered.

"Hi! Muddy Face! Keep you waiting?" He gave the hand with the ring a quick squeeze.

"No. I had to stay after school." She made her voice sound like a small girl's. "I been bein' scolded."

Cleve chuckled. He turned her hand and twisted the diamond around into the sunlight where the facets splintered into rainbow lights. "Like it?" he asked.

"Love it. It's gorgeous, Cleve. Much too elegant for the likes of me. I'd have been satisfied with—well, with nothing—just you. But you *and* Gibraltar! What more could a girl want?"

"A plain band might be nice." His voice sounded wistful. "Cleve to Torrey, June—"

"O-ooo! Not June. June's here right now. It's too soon, Cleve. It takes a while to get ready. You have to come home and meet my family. And I have to finish up a whale of a lot of work. I have papers and finals and—count 'em—two stories to learn." Her voice rose in a wail. "You don't know what that means. Hours and hours of agony."

Cleve pulled her to her feet and they started off across campus. "Why do you bother, Torrey? As soon as I get a job we'll be married."

She considered this. "Nope. I have to see it through. You can't start something and not finish it.
10

Mom and Dad wouldn't like it. That little Jordan beast won't let me off. He told me today. Get those stories—or else! Do you know what else he said?"

Cleve grinned down at her in anticipation, watching her dark eyes squint like Dr. Jordan, the dimple in her cheek flickering as she pursed her lips. Torrey had a trick of lifting one eyebrow that gave her face a comical look. She began to stroke her chin between thumb and fingers.

"He said, I'll have you know, that I had a certain amount of pulchritude!"

Cleve gave a snort. "Observing cuss. But that's what that ring's for, Torrey Thorne. It says you're mine—all mine. You tell that undersized gorilla hands off. Or I'll gr-r-r-r-ind his bones to make my bread!"

Torrey stopped in the path. "Oh, Cleve, could you? That would solve everything!"

They shouted with laughter, oblivious of the passing students.

"I almost forgot," Cleve went on. "I have an invitation for you. Gang wants to meet you. I told her we'd be there for dinner tomorrow night."

"Oh, Cleve, I can't. I mustn't. I need to spend every spare minute on stories."

Cleve frowned. "You don't understand, Torrey," he said soberly. "Gang is my family. We pretty much have to do as she wants. At least this year and next. I don't get a cent of my own money until then. Before that Gang holds the purse strings."

"It sounds as though you're afraid of her, Cleve."

"I'm not exactly afraid of her"—Cleve's voice was cautious—"but, believe me, I don't underestimate her."

11

"What if she doesn't like me, Cleve?" Torrey's voice was taut with worry. "What then?"

"Oh, she will," he said easily. "And I'll get a job to make sure. If we have to starve for a while, I don't know of a nicer person than Torrey Thorne to do it with."

Torrey was unhappy. "I can work too, Cleve. At least if I get this degree, I can. But I don't want to be the one coming between you and Miss Clevinger."

She didn't want Cluney Mary Clevinger coming between her and Cleve either, Torrey was thinking.

They crossed a foot bridge over a chuckling stream. They were alone on a path between tall shrubs with spicy shell-pink flowers. Cleve looked back. "Good! Nobody in sight!"

He put his hands on either side of her head. His gray eyes looked deep into her brown ones. "Your eyes are the same color as a shaded trout stream, Torrey Thorne, and your hair has gold lights like the mica on the bottom of the pool."

"Fool's gold," said Torrey.

Cleve laughed. "You know something, Torrey? I've laughed more with you these last few weeks than I ever laughed in my life before." He pushed back her hair. Then he crushed her to him, his hands hard on her shoulder blades. "You're so funny and so darn sweet."

"You too, Cleve." Her voice was muffled against his shoulder.

They heard footsteps on the bridge and separated.

"I can't get over how we found each other," he said when they were alone again. "Here I was, all ready to take off for South America—shots, visa, and

12

everything. Then I met you. Just think if I hadn't gone to the Wolf Ridge Square Dance. I almost didn't."

"I know. I nearly didn't too."

"The minute you took your place in the set that night, I knew, Torrey, didn't you?"

Torrey didn't want to admit she hadn't known. She and Kate had driven down to Wolf Ridge in Torrey's battered car. Cleve had been just another partner whirling her with an expert hand when they met, stepping off to the quick calls. He had stayed beside her when they stopped, flushed and panting, to rest on the lawn. The ground was damp, and she had taken off one flat-heeled shoe to scrape away the mud. As she brushed the hair off her hot face, she had left a black smear across it.

Cleve Macklin had laughed at her. "Muddy Face!" he taunted. "Here's my handkerchief."

She was pleased when he sought her out because he was tall and clean-cut, with merry eyes and a ready laugh. But she hadn't realized that she had made a conquest until he called her the next day and every day, until the dates were interfering with her college work. In two weeks he was the most important thing in Torrey Thorne's life. There didn't seem to be hours enough to hold Cleve Macklin and a degree in Library Science at the same time.

"You've tangled up my career like fury, Mr. Macklin."

"I couldn't care less. Your career from now on, Miss Thorne, is me. We won't tell Gang we met at a hoe-down. We'll tell her we met at Carey's. We did, the next week, remember?"

There it was again. Why shouldn't they tell Miss

Cluney Mary Clevinger where they had met? Torrey could see that what his godmother thought was important—really important—mattered to Cleve. She was surprised at her own reaction. It's almost as though I were jealous, she thought. It was ridiculous to be jealous of an old woman three times her age. But Torrey knew she was. She was jealous of a woman she had never met, whose opinions mattered to Cleve Macklin. Almost as much as Torrey Thorne's mattered. Or maybe more? She realized that it wasn't only jealousy that stirred in her. It was fear as well.

"I don't see how I can go tomorrow, Cleve. I'm swamped."

"I don't see how we can't. I told Gang we'd be there. If I told her you couldn't—wouldn't—come, well, I don't think she'd appreciate it, that's all. I'd hate to get us off on the wrong foot with anybody like Gang."

"Even if she knew I had exes and papers and things like that? Wouldn't she understand?"

Cleve twisted his fingers in hers as they walked along the path. "Gang wants to meet you, Torrey. I haven't exactly told her we're engaged, but she knows you mean a lot to me. It was her own idea, having us to dinner. If you wear the ring, she'll know that we're serious."

Torrey stopped. "You mean—*Cleve*! We can't just spring it like that! She'd have every right to be upset."

Cleve looked cross. "Well, I'm not going to tell her ahead of time, that's flat. When she sees that ring, she'll know it's all settled. Just keep it out of sight until she thaws out."

Torrey was appalled. This was going against the grain. Against all her upbringing, all of her innate honesty. Cleve didn't feel about it as she did. She could see that. He was afraid of Miss Cluney Mary Clevinger, and to him this seemed the easiest way around that fear.

Torrey was afraid too. But she wanted the announcement of her engagement to be a matter of pride, of dignity. She wanted Cleve to share this news with his people, as she expected to share it with hers.

An ugly little doubt reared its head in Torrey's mind. Was she prouder of Cleve than he was of her? Was he feeling apologetic about Torrey Thorne to Miss Cluney Mary Clevinger?

Torrey flung her head up in a quick gesture. But as she opened her lips to protest, Cleve Macklin closed them with his own. In the wave of emotion that swept over her Torrey knew that nothing else mattered—nothing.

3

Torrey worked hard that night at the library until it closed. She finished the paper on Public Relations. She wasn't satisfied with it, but there was no more time. She still had the typing to do.

The last ten minutes she spent frantically poring over the three books of myths she had been able to find. All the familiar ones had been given in class. Dr. Jordan didn't want them repeated.

"If you all tell different stories," he had said, "you will become familiar with many more than you could prepare for yourselves. In that way you are bound to find many that others have chosen that will have special appeal for you as well."

He was right, of course. But as she leafed through the books, Torrey hated the thought of him. "Thor's Journey to Jotenheim," "Iduna and the Golden Apples," "Atalanta," "The Golden Touch." All the ones she knew had been done. She picked up the book of Hawaiian myths. The pictures were lovely, and the words were full of beauty. Torrey knew that two months ago she would have plunged joyously into

better to see Miss Cluney Mary some other time?"

"No. This is vital. If it works out, we'll have some pretty important decisions to make. I need you there. It's your future as well as mine. I'll get down as soon as I can. Dinner's at seven."

"How do I dress, Cleve?"

"Dress? I don't know. You always look good to me. Wear that mustard thing with the red belt."

"Where will you be all day?"

"I'm meeting this friend of Gang's at the Fairmont. It looks like a break, Torrey. I don't know much about it yet, but it looks big—real big. See you then. Don't forget, Muddy Face, I love you."

Torrey turned away from the phone at the boarding house with a deep sense of impending trouble, which increased as she realized she would be late to Dr. Jordan's class.

He frowned as she barged in. Henrietta Mert was up on her feet, already launched on a story.

Torrey pushed her way across a whole row of students to the one empty seat. As she sat down she dropped a book with a spanking bang.

"Just a moment, Miss Mert." Dr. Jordan's voice was squeaky with irritation. He teetered on his feet, stroking his beard and glaring at Torrey. "Ordinarily I welcome interruptions for my storytellers. You will have them many times during your careers, and your recovery is a measure of your poise. But I can see no excuse for the sort of interruption to which we have just been subjected."

Torrey felt her face flame as she bent down to pick up her book, dropping a pencil as she straightened up. "Sorry," she mumbled as she reached for the pencil.

Torrey listened with growing horror as Henrietta's lush voice calmly disclosed the basic facts about the wedding of Thetis and Peleus. Torrey couldn't believe her ears. Henrietta was telling the story of "The Apple of Discord," the story she had tried so hard to learn that morning.

When Henrietta had dispassionately and efficiently launched the siege of Troy, she sat down to the sound of pattering hands. Everyone always clapped for Henrietta. She seemed to expect it.

"Thank you, Miss Mert." Dr. Jordan's voice sounded tired, tired of people telling stories like Henrietta Mert. Torrey stiffened as his eye caught hers. "Have you a story to offer us this morning, Miss Thorne?"

Torrey was still in a state of shock. She couldn't bear to admit to Dr. Jordan that her story had just been told. It would sound like a trumped-up alibi. Worse than that, he might tell her to go ahead with it, for the purposes of comparison. He had done that before. The comparison would be pitiful. Torrey knew that she hadn't put enough time on the story. She didn't have Henrietta's photographic memory. She had planned to tell the story in her own words. She knew what Dr. Jordan would say. Slipshod storytelling, he would call it.

"No, I haven't a story for this morning, Dr. Jordan," she answered.

He eyed her for several seconds, his lips tight. Torrey quailed under his level look. The whole class squirmed. He made a mark in his little black book. "Miss Hart."

He listened with badly concealed impatience to the saccharine Christmas story called "The Disappointed Reindeer." He ripped both story and story-teller to bits at its conclusion.

"A Christmas story," he said, "should reflect our joy, should express our wonder over the miracle of birth. Our songs, our carols, our manger scenes are a part of that rejoicing. Silly tales of Santa Claus, of reindeer, of little lambs, told in a sentimental fashion, are out of place."

Torrey bit her lip. She thought if Miss Hart liked the story, didn't that give it a certain virtue? Hasn't he been telling us all term we must pick out stories we like ourselves? He could have said all that tactfully and still have given her credit for a story well learned. He's mean—he's downright mean.

The owl-eyed young man in back of Torrey unexpectedly came through with "The Storyteller" by Saki, where the wolf ate up the very good little girl, all but her shoes and the three clinking good-conduct medals. It wasn't the kind of story to appeal to Henrietta Mert or to Miss Hart, but it tickled Torrey and, to her surprise, Dr. Jordan.

He was still laughing when he turned back to his notes. "I have a blow for the students who must tell last-minute stories to children. St. Mary's Playground will be closed for the rest of this week. I have made arrangements for stories with the Child Welfare people for tonight. They will have children there for stories between seven and eight o'clock. It is the only time I can be there. Which of you can go? Will you, Miss Thorne?"

This was her chance to redeem herself. She wouldn't even have to learn a story. She could tell the Greek myth she had learned that morning. This would settle it once and for all. Then she heard

21

Cleve's voice over the phone: "This is really vital, Torrey. Dinner's at seven."

"I—I can't go tonight, Dr. Jordan."

"You have a final this week?"

"No." She was grasping at straws. "But I have a paper to type for Dr. Stern."

"That paper isn't due until Friday," Henrietta's mellow voice boomed out.

"I think you had better sandwich the library paper in between now and Friday, Miss Thorne. A story takes only a few minutes to tell. We can let you retire to your typing as soon as you are through. This is the last opportunity I can offer for those of you who need to tell one more story to children."

Torrey didn't answer. Again she lowered her eyes, tracing the letters on her notebook with a careful pencil, hiding the sick feeling inside of her. This was her last chance.

She could hear Cleve's urgent voice. "I need you there, Torrey. If it works out, we'll have some pretty important decisions to make. This can mean our whole future."

It was a straight choice. On the one hand, there was the degree she had worked so hard to get and which she needed, no matter what the future had to offer. On the other hand, there was Cleve and a strange woman whom Torrey had never met, a woman who held Cleve's future, and now Torrey Thorne's future, in her sixty-year-old fingers.

As she thought of Miss Cluney Mary Clevinger, the jealousy inside of her swept everything before it, and Torrey made her choice.

She raised her eyes. "I'm sorry, Dr. Jordan. I can't possibly make it tonight."

At his cold stare of incredulity, Torrey looked down again at the aimless penciling on her notebook, her thumb pressed hard against the diamond in her palm.

4

Torrey dressed with care for the dinner with Miss Clevinger. She hesitated between the mustard dress that Cleve liked and a navy silk suit that she had worn for two years. With the short jacket off, the slim sheath could double for a cocktail dress. With some clips borrowed from Kate, it would look festive. Not knowing what to expect of this date, she chose the suit.

She was glad when Kate decided to drive down with her to visit her married sister in Marysdale.

"I can't study any more!" Kate groaned. "My brain is ready to pop. I'll go down and relax at Nora's. It's such a madhouse down there that I forget my troubles. Five children and two boxers and a Siamese cat and Granny. All yowling at once, and it's kind of restful. Besides, you oughtn't to be driving around alone at night in that rickety heap."

It was a sparkling afternoon, with the late sun glinting on the restless water. Torrey would have enjoyed the ride across the bridge and down the freeway along the shore if her mind had not been so churned up over Cleve.

"You're awful quiet, Macushla," Kate commented, drawing the visors down against the sun. "Love or trouble?"

"Both, I'm afraid. By coming down here tonight to have dinner with Cleve's godmother, I'll flunk Jordan's class."

"You sure?"

"Yep."

"Well, if you marry Cleve—and it looks like it with that ring—do you care?"

"I care like fury."

"Maybe Jordan'll remember how bright you were to begin with."

"No hope. He gave us fair warning. But I couldn't give up this date."

"Godmother that important?"

"She's Cluney Mary Clevinger."

Kate whistled.

"She has a big place down the Peninsula, Kate, near your sister's. Know it?"

"Sure. Everybody knows it. She owns half the town and keeps it in wild oats and oak trees. She won't sell an acre or give a right of way or build a road through. Nora's young ones have to take a bus to school around miles of red-brick wall. Nora says Cluney Mary has a special parking place in front of the Presbyterian church. No one would think of taking it. If there's standing room only inside, nobody sits in *her* pew."

"What does she look like?"

"Like an elongated horse."

"Sounds gruesome. I'm scared of her, Kate, and I think Cleve is, too."

Kate snorted. "I wouldn't think you scared that easily."

"You're not marrying Cleve."

Torrey concentrated on traffic until she was safely up on the maze of overpasses looking down on the City. "Have you ever been inside the Clevinger place, Kate?"

"Not to speak of. We used to climb the fence when we were young and reckless and steal sour plums off her trees. The antipathy of the gardener made it exciting enough to be worth-while."

"What's it like?"

"Crazy. The big house burned down years and years ago. It was tremendous, fifty rooms they say, all turrets and balconies and gingerbread. It was built in the sixties when the big land grabs were on. The Clevingers went to Europe and sent back shiploads of junk. Fireplaces and statues and tapestries and paintings. Whole parquet floors and fountains, even."

"When did it burn?"

" 'Way back. Before my time."

"Didn't they rebuild?"

"Not the big house. The old gentleman had two hobbies. Books and flowers. He had built a special place to house his books away from the big house, a kind of hexagonal room lined with books. Running off in two wings were glass houses full of orchids and rhododendrons and things. The Clevingers were away when the house burned. The shock was too much for the old man."

"Is that where Cluney Mary lives now?"

"More or less. It's been changed a lot. Her grand-mother roofed over the glass wings and moved in all the junk that was hauled out of the big house at the time of the fire. It's been built onto until it's a rabbit warren."

"Does she live there all alone?"

"Except for servants. She opens it once a year for a big church tea. Everybody goes, just to see the house. Nora says it's weird. Decapitated statues sitting around with their heads in their laps. Books from the floor to the ceiling."

"How did Cluney Mary get it?"

"Well, the grandmother had one son, and he married a woman she couldn't stand. Rumor has it she paid them to live down South some place. They had one child, Cluney Mary. She pleased the old lady and got the whole works."

"Didn't she ever marry?"

"Cluney Mary? No. She had a bang-up coming-out ball and engagement party. A real hullabaloo. Caterers and marquee and what-all. Then World War One came along, and the old lady put her foot down on their getting married. The war would be over in a month or two, she said. He was killed in France."

For the first time Torrey felt a kinship with Miss Cluney Mary Clevinger. Perhaps Miss Cluney Mary had loved this young soldier the way Torrey loved Cleve. Would she give up marriage forever if Cleve went off to war? Yes, she would. But she wouldn't let him go, she thought fiercely, without marrying him before he went.

Then another thought struck her. Maybe all that heartbreak had warped Miss Clevinger. Maybe she wouldn't want Cleve to marry anyone. And if she didn't, would Cleve marry Torrey Thorne if Miss Cluney Mary put her foot down? Torrey wasn't sure.

"I don't know how she gets such a hold on Cleve," she told Kate, watching a car tooling in from a merging lane. "He says she has control of his money."

"Well, he's not feeble, is he? Can't he earn some by himself?"

"We both can," said Torrey. Maybe Cleve was making plans right now, with the friend of Miss Cluney Mary's, to earn money. He had said it was important. Their whole future, he had said. But as she looked out over the dancing whitecaps on the bay, Torrey shivered. I've put all my eggs in one basket, she was thinking.

She dropped Kate off at Nora's and turned up the tree-lined avenue that led along the ivy-covered red-stone fence of the Clevinger estate. There were no sidewalks. The road turned out now and then to miss a big oak or elm. Behind high gates Torrey caught glimpses of shady, winding drives, across from the stone fence, that gave a maximum of privacy. She passed a carefully tended golf course, a stable, and grazing fields before she reached the imposing gates that Cleve had pointed out to her.

Torrey drove a long way between plowed fields under old oaks. She passed a block of eucalyptus trees, tall and pastel-skinned, with shreds of bark hanging in strips from naked limbs, their sickle leaves drooping. Beyond a second gate there were lawns and shrubs and fountains.

As Torrey found a place to park, she looked around for Cleve's convertible. Behind a hedge of lilacs she could see an oval swimming pool, placid and calm in the evening light. But there were no other cars beside her own.

"Well, here goes!" she muttered, pulling on her white gloves.

The door was opened by a chunky woman in black, with an impassive face and unquiet hands.

"Miss Thorne?" The voice was flat and uninterested.

"Yes. Good evening." Cleve hadn't told Torrey much about Miss Cluney Mary or anyone else in the household. She wasn't sure who this was.

"Miss Cluney Mary's engaged at present," said the flat voice. "I'm Mrs. Jones. Carmelita Jones. Let me take your bag."

Torrey stripped off her gloves and slipped them under the flap of her purse. There's a smell to this house, she was thinking, a smell of what? Old wood? Old people?

There was a confusion of sound from somewhere. She followed Mrs. Jones across an unlit hall where a narrow circular staircase wound upward into darkness. As Mrs. Jones snapped on the light in a small reception room, the formal chill struck Torrey unpleasantly.

There was one chair of elaborately carved teak, a small love seat in the same twisted pattern of coiled dragons, a heavy marble-topped table, its pedestal carved and curlicued. The walls and floor were bare. The drapes at the one window were of heavy wine-colored velour, reaching from the high ceiling to the floor. A huge hydrangea bush in the garden shut out the view. It was a place to wait.

Torrey turned to Mrs. Jones. "Is Cleve—is Mr. Macklin here?"

There was a flicker of surprise in Mrs. Jones' opaque eyes as she rubbed her hands down her hips. "Didn't he tell you? Mr. Cleve won't be here."

"Won't *be* here?" There was more than a flicker of surprise in Torrey's voice. There was consternation.

"No. Mr. Cleve has other plans this evening. Er— Miss Cluney Mary'll explain it all. She's in the library now, watching the last of the fights with Pierre—he's the cook. By the sounds of it, the fight's about over. I couldn't ask her out before it's settled one way or the other. If you'll excuse me—with Pierre in there—I'll have to see about the dinner."

Torrey sat down on the edge of the love seat. The confusion of sound, she realized, was the screaming and yelling over the TV as the fight went on. It was cold in the small, bare room. Torrey wished she had worn something warmer than the silk suit.

Where was Cleve? Why hadn't he let her know he wouldn't be here? Why had he let her in for something like this? What were the other plans? Who was this friend of Miss Cluney Mary Clevinger who could keep Cleve from a date as important as this one?

The minutes dragged by as she worried, until a slow anger began to seethe in Torrey. Cleve had no right to do this to her. Miss Cluney Mary had no right to ignore her arrival. A hostess had no right to shunt a guest off into a bleak, elegant little room while she listened to a TV fight with the cook.

Then a miserable thought came along to sit beside the others. Torrey Thorne had no right to become engaged to Cleve Macklin before she had worked out some of these problems with her own family, and with Cleve's.

Torrey didn't know how long she sat there. It seemed hours. Then a door opened. There was laughter, and a thick masculine voice, *"C'est bon, non?"* Torry heard limping footsteps. A tall, bony woman stood in the doorway, her long face still wrinkled with laughter, which congealed to a blank look of unbelief as her eyes fastened on the diamond ring on Torrey's hand.

Torrey rose to her feet, her head high. For a split second the tall girl in the bare and unfriendly room and the taller woman in the doorway stood facing each other. Torrey saw a woman who looked nearly six feet tall, with straight white hair pulled back from a long, tanned face. Her dark, sunken eyes must have been beautiful years before. Torrey remembered Kate's description, "Like an elongated horse." Miss Cluney Mary was dressed in a brown tweed suit loosely hung from broad shoulders. She wore thick stockings and highly polished brown Oxfords. Her clothes looked as if she had been born in them. In one hand she carried a gnarled and polished cane.

Torrey was conscious of her own flimsy silk suit and heels. But most of all, she was conscious of the big diamond flashing on her finger.

Miss Cluney Mary came forward. "It was kind of you to come all this way at the request of an old woman, Miss Thorne. It's been a beautiful day for a drive, hasn't it?"

Beautiful, nothing! thought Torrey angrily. I've thrown away a degree for—this! She held out a hesitant hand.

Miss Cluney Mary ignored it. "Come in, my dear. We'll have dinner and talk things over."

Miss Cluney Mary, Mrs. Jones, and Torrey entered a big dining room. Torrey figured that the table must be at least fifteen feet long. It was of dark and light inlaid wood, with Italian place mats. Old, ornate silver and heavy cut glass winked in the candlelight that shed a small, glimmering pool of light at one end, while the rest of the bare table stretched away into the gloom.

Mrs. Jones served the tasteless meal of salad and cold cuts and then ice cream and "boughten" cookies.

Torrey couldn't help wondering what the cook did besides listen to the fights. Then she grinned to herself. Anything that had been served, she realized, would have tasted like sawdust.

Miss Clevinger kept the conversation going with a series of questions. Torrey wanted to ask about Cleve, but she felt tongue-tied.

"You graduated from the College of the Pacific, and now you are at Libr'ry School, Miss Thorne? You plan to become a librarian, is that it? You like books, I take it, and you read a great deal?"

Torrey laughed a little. "Librarians like books, but they can't read all of them."

"That accounts for so many poorly written books on our libr'ry shelves, perhaps?" The voice of the older woman was cutting.

Torrey winced. "We have to cater to all kinds of tastes, all kinds of needs, Miss Clevinger."

"And most of the taste for libr'ry books being bad, you cater to that?"

Torrey was stung. Why do I defend their taste, she

wondered, when I won't even be one of them? She decided to change the subject. "I had planned to be working with children. I like children and books and storytelling."

"Storytelling?"

"Yes. It's an important way to introduce children to books, a way to get them into libraries."

"Times have changed. We couldn't wait to be old enough to get into books and libr'ries in my day. We didn't require bait. I suppose it is all television and radio now."

"Libraries use those media sometimes to help get children interested in books." Good heavens, she thought, I sound like Dr. Jordan himself.

"Your home is in the San Joaquin Valley, I understand? Your people farm? What sort of farming?"

"We have grapes and olives and figs."

"Sounds rather biblical."

Torrey laughed. Talking about her own home and the ranch had put her at ease. "Sometimes the olives pull us through. Sometimes the figs."

"Do you plan to go back to the San Joaquin Valley to do your library work?"

Torrey wanted to say, I won't be doing library work. I'm marrying Cleve Macklin. But the words stuck in her throat. "I'm not sure what my plans are," she answered. The reserve in Torrey's voice snapped the thread of easy conversation between them.

When the meal was over, Miss Cluney Mary rose from the table and took Torrey's arm. "As you see, I am a little lame. Come see my begonias."

She led Torrey out into the garden, pausing to go down the stone steps one at a time. They followed a twisting path of flagstones to the tiled swimming pool, reflecting the setting sun in its still, turquoise depths.

"It's lovely!" Torrey exclaimed.

"It's a luxury, an extravagance," answered Miss Cluney Mary sharply. "I never use it. I have to keep the place fenced because of it. It's a hideous hole in the ground, empty. It's a catch-all for leaves and trash when it's full."

"Couldn't you let people use it? Church people or youth groups?"

"Ha! Have you ever let people into your grounds where you live? They trampled the begonias and left gum wrappers and cartons all over the place. Do you have a pool on your ranch? It would be of more use over there in the heat, I should think."

"A sort of pool," Torrey answered honestly. "It's an irrigation basin, really. But it's cold and wet and deep enough for swimming."

Miss Cluney Mary had lost interest. She pointed to the bank of begonias. Huge flowers of lemon and flame raised heavy waxen heads above thick green leaves.

"They're lovely," said Torrey again. But her own enthusiasm had cooled in the face of Miss Cluney Mary's indifference to her opinion.

"They're all in pots," explained Miss Cluney Mary. "When they have finished blooming, the gardener takes them out and stores them. He sets out autumn plants, shower chrysanthemums, usually."

Torrey was thinking how simple and easy it was to create beauty if you had money enough.

When they returned to the house, Torrey helped Miss Cluney Mary up the steps.

"Thank you, my dear. It's pleasant to have a young person's strength to lean upon."

It was the first warm thing she had said, Torrey thought.

Mrs. Jones met them as they came in. "A long-distance for you, Miss Cluney Mary, from the city."

"Thank you."

Torrey would have held back, but Miss Cluney Mary drew her into the library with her. "I won't be long. Sit here." She all but pushed Torrey into a chair close to the telephone.

The strangely shaped room was lined with books. Every inch of wall between windows and doors was solidly packed with them, set after set in expensive, tooled-leather bindings. There was too much furniture, heavy carved pieces that seemed too big for the room. There were several more-than-life-sized statues, a winged Mercury racing in full flight, a headless seated woman of white marble holding a lovely classical head in her lap, a bronze Moor complete with a gold coin necklace.

This was all that Torrey saw before her attention was riveted on the phone.

"Oh, Clevinger! My dear, dear boy!"

Torrey had turned the diamond into her palm and she realized that it was soaking wet. She tried to sit at ease, but her back was stiff with tension, with fear.

"What is your decision then? Good! Good! I hoped you would, of course. Yes. Yes, indeed. He is, isn't he? Dynamic! Yes. Hmmm. Oh, yes, I knew you'd feel that. Well. I'm glad it's settled."

What was settled? Who was dynamic? What had been decided? Torrey was seething.

"No. It's too bad. I should have liked to have seen you both, of course. But it would be stupid—simply stupid—not to go. Yes. Yes, she's here. Just one moment. Good-bye, dear, dear boy. Good-bye. Write when you can."

Torrey was on her feet, her heart pounding, her knees half jelled. "Cleve!" All her anger and fear and frustration melted at the sound of his voice. Out of the corner of her eye Torrey saw Miss Cluney Mary sit down close at hand. But it didn't matter. Nothing mattered but that Cleve's warm and loving voice was in her ear once more.

"Torrey, darling! How's it going?"

"All right, Cleve." And so it was, Torrey thought, her heart singing. Everything was all right. But it wasn't.

"Torrey, I've some tremendous news for you. It's too good to be true. You know how I've fretted and fumed these last few weeks?"

Torrey didn't know. She hadn't any idea he had been fretting and fuming. "But—" she began.

"Listen, Torrey. It's a tremendous break. Remember I told you about the shots and visa and things? This friend of Gang's is here. Just for today. He's leaving for South America tonight. He's taking me with him."

"He's—what?"

"I'm at the airport now. We're leaving on the plane in a few minutes. For Santiago. He owns all sorts of things down there, mines and business property and —oh, Lord! it's hard to take it all in, right off. Anyway, he says he needs a corporation lawyer for a year or two. He likes me, and I like him. I've been all day racing around getting things okayed."

36

Torrey was stunned. "Cleve!" There was heartbreak in that one word. Then she caught sight of Miss Cluney Mary's long, bony face, her bright eyes in their dark purple sockets fastened on Torrey. Torrey's head went up with a jerk. "It sounds fabulous!" she said in a brittle voice.

"Oh, it is! It's the chance of a lifetime. Getting in like this, with no experience."

"Wonderful!"

"Listen, darling."

Did he think for one minute she wasn't listening? Torrey forced out a chuckle through stiff lips, as warm as she could make it.

"As soon as I find a place for us to live and get straightened away, you're to come down. We'll be married down there, Torrey, okay?"

She started to say, I'll have to think that over. I'll give this old woman something to think over, she thought grimly. "I'll come whenever you say the word, Cleve."

"There's the last call for the plane!" Cleve's voice was full of suppressed excitement.

"Bon voyage, Cleve. Where is it—Chile?"

"Remember, Muddy Face, I love you!"

Torrey hung up with the sound of his kiss smacking in her ear. Take it on the chin, Torrey Thorne, she told herself. Don't give this old woman the satisfaction of knowing what a knockout this is. She turned around on the telephone stool. "Cleve is as excited as a small boy with a new popgun," she said brightly.

Miss Cluney Mary's voice reproved this levity. "Clevinger has much more in his fist than a popgun,

Miss Thorne. I'm so very, very happy that it has worked out so well."

I'll bet, thought Torrey.

"Now I think you and I should talk things over," Miss Cluney Mary went on. "That is the reason I wanted you to come here tonight."

I wish I hadn't, thought Torrey. I wish to heaven I hadn't. Her mind was turning and twisting through the maze of consequences she was now facing. It would have turned out the same way whether I came or not, she was thinking. This elongated horse has enough money, enough influence to remove me like a begonia pot, and I'm being torn up by the roots in the process.

"I feel that it is important, Miss Thorne," the inexorable voice went on, "that Clevinger should take this big chance that has come his way—unencumbered."

Torrey's eyes blazed in a stricken face. But she held her tongue.

"It is fair to neither one of you to have him go off for a year—even more, perhaps—tied to something —to anyone—bound by a hasty decision that he will probably—shall we say—outgrow in the meantime."

"Why should he?"

"It is inevitable, don't you think? Clevinger led a fairly sheltered life here. Oh, he sowed a few wild oats at Stanford. He spent an interim period in the Air Corps. Then he buckled down to his Bar examinations. It is time for him to launch out into his career." Miss Cluney Mary hesitated, frowning. Then she raised her hands, bony, deeply tanned hands, in a gesture of impatience. "Now he thinks he has fallen in love with the first pretty girl he has met."

"I don't think it was quite like that." Torrey's eyes looked with level directness into those of the older woman.

But was it? They had met in a whirl of folk dancing, as gay as peasant stitching. Cleve had rushed her off her feet, and in a few weeks they were engaged. Was she his first girl? Torrey doubted that. But she didn't really know Cleve Macklin. She could see that. All the time that she had thought he was as absorbed in her as she was in him, he had been fuming and fretting, champing at the bit, anxious to be up and off about the business of getting a start in life.

"Cleve and I are engaged to be married." Torrey kept her tense voice quiet and even. "I didn't think we should—so soon—but Cleve did. He gave me this ring as a pledge." Torrey held out her hand. The big diamond winked and glittered on her slender finger.

"Yes!" The old woman's voice was harsh. "He had no right—no right—" she stopped. Her long, knobby fingers drummed on the chair arm. She seemed to gather her forces. "Miss Thorne, that ring belonged to my dearest friend. Clevinger's mother was more like a sister, a part of my family. I was heartbroken at her death."

Torrey waited, sitting on the telephone stool, her hands quiet in her lap.

"Mary Macklin left her little boy in my care," Miss Cluney Mary was saying. "I raised him as I would have raised a child of my own. I feel that his mother's ring was placed in my trust, just as he was."

Torrey clenched her fists. "Cleve said it was to be his engagement ring, and we were engaged." What

39

made her say "were"? "We *are* engaged," she added stubbornly.

The older woman's voice was reasonable, detached. "Clevinger will meet all sorts of women in Santiago, Miss Thorne. Sophisticated and cosmopolitan, on the one hand, protected and mysterious, on the other. Don't you think it might be wiser to set him free to find out where his real feelings lie, either for you or for someone else? Or would you prefer to wait and let him write you later for that —freedom of choice—and the ring?"

Torrey stared at the implacable face of Cluney Mary Clevinger. You devil, she thought, you wicked, inhuman old devil! She thought suddenly of Dr. Jordan and the choice she had made in his class. This was a harder choice. The day before, she had chosen Cleve. Now, she knew, that choosing had been a delusion. Others were doing the choosing. Cleve had chosen to go off to South America, and this hard-shelled old woman had chosen to send him there.

She rose to her feet. "Put that way, I haven't much choice." She stripped the ring from her finger, dropping it into Miss Cluney Mary's outstretched hand. "The ring itself doesn't matter," she said, her eyes bright. "I would gladly have been pledged to Cleve without it. But with or without the ring, until I hear otherwise from him, I still consider myself engaged."

Miss Cluney Mary slid the ring on her own bony finger. She drew a deep breath. "That is for you young people to decide. It was good of you to come, Miss Thorne. I appreciate it. You will excuse me now, I know. My knee troubles me after a long day. Jones!"

Mrs. Jones appeared with Torrey's bag and gloves, like a rabbit out of a hat, thought Torrey. Miss Cluney Mary put her hand on Mrs. Jones' arm. Torrey followed them out into the hall, brilliantly lit now from a chandelier of cut-glass pendants. At the foot of the stairs a chair with arms outstretched was waiting, facing across the steps. Miss Cluney Mary seated herself in the chair. Mrs. Jones pushed a button. The chair slid slowly up the stairs on a smooth track, swinging around the curve of the stair-case. As the chair reached the last of the curve, Miss Cluney Mary raised her hand in a careless gesture of dismissal. The diamond winked and sparkled in the strong light.

How bitter a thing it is to look into happiness
through another man's eyes

WILLIAM SHAKESPEARE—AS YOU LIKE IT

5

TORREY FOUND KATE at her sister's house in the midst of a happy hubbub, trying to get three reluctant children into night clothes.

"Catch that hellion!" yelled Kate as one small boy dodged out the front door.

Torrey caught a glimpse of the living room, where the two boxers were frantically barking. A Siamese cat was sitting in a litter of papers on top of the grand piano, eyeing the confusion with virtuous blue eyes.

"Listen, you kids," shouted Kate. "This is Torrey Thorne. She's the best storyteller you ever heard, barrin' Granny. You get busy and wash your teeth and hop in, and she'll tell you the story of 'The Gunniwolf.'"

"What's a gunnawoof?" demanded the small boy Torrey was clutching.

"You get into bed and I'll tell you," she answered, turning him around and giving his fat little rump a smart pat.

The children all pushed their way into a bathroom together. There were yells of fury, the sound of things landing on the tiled floor.

"Don't worry," said Kate, handing Torrey a brush and some toothpaste, "everything's plastic. Sorry to rake you in on this, Torrey, I didn't think you'd be back so soon. I told Nora to take the two oldest to the movies. She can't get out much, with Bob gone."

"That's all right," answered Torrey, busy smearing toothpaste on a frazzled brush. She was glad of the chance to turn her mind from thoughts of a plane heading out across the bay into the night.

The children scampered into a large bedroom that seemed to be literally filled with beds. They scrambled into three of them. Kate went around tucking in covers, kissing damp faces that were freshly washed but unwiped.

Torrey sat on an empty bed while Kate snapped off the switch. Light filtered in from the hall, showing the white beds with blobs of dark faces against their pillows.

"Go on!" said an impatient voice. "Tell the one about the gunnisack."

"I want 'Goldilocks.' Do you know the story of 'Goldilocks'?"

"Everybody settle down," said Torrey. She felt relaxed for the first time in days. There was no room in her heart for anything but a story for three tired, excited children.

Kate plunked down beside her and stretched out, spread-eagled on the bed. "Go on!" she mimicked.

"Once upon a time," began Torrey slowly, "there was a little girl who lived close to the edge of the jungle."

She was surprised at the magic and mystery created in her own mood by those ancient words. "Have a 'Once upon a time' quality to your opening words," Dr. Jordan had said, "no matter what they say."

He had also said, she remembered, "If you once learn 'The Gunniwolf' you will have a story at your tongue tip that can be used for all ages." She had learned it at once. Its rhythmic pattern made it easy to learn. It was a story of suspense, of laughter—based, she suspected, on a little, delicious fear.

"The little girl promised she wouldn't go near the jungle." Were there jungles in Chile? Torrey had heard of mines, high mountains, fertilizer, copper. That was all she knew of Chile, and nothing at all of Santiago.

The story of "The Gunniwolf" had the great virtue of being easily remembered. It could be told effectively with very little mental effort. As the wolf woke up and came after the little girl—"Hunkacha, Hunkacha, Hunkacha"—Torrey could think about Dr. Jordan, about the patterns of stories, even about a silver plane, with lights blinking, winging its way south in the summer night.

"Then you sing that guten, sweeten song again." I'm like the little girl, Torrey was thinking. Venturing onto forbidden ground. And the gunniwolf was an old woman in a tweed suit, with dark, sunken eyes and a lame knee. Torrey had had no 'guten, sweeten song' to lull the gunniwolf, and the old woman had snapped her up like the wolf in the Saki story had eaten that too good little girl, all but her shoes and good-conduct medals. Not even any good-conduct medals, Torrey was thinking.

"And then the little girl ran as fast as ever she

could, pit-pat, pit-pat, pit-pat," breathed Torrey, "until she got to the edge of the jungle." I'm still in the jungle, she was thinking. "Pit-pat, pit-pat, pitty-pat, pit-tee-pat, until she got to her very own door-step."

Torrey paused. "The pause is a very effective part of your story," Dr. Jordan had said. "It must be timed with skill. Learn to use it and it will heighten the dramatic effect."

"And she *never* went *near* the jungle again," concluded Torrey with laughter in her voice.

The silence that followed was flattering. Then one small voice piped up, "Wasn't she a naughty gwirrell!"

A deep masculine voice from the middle bed said, with relish, "That ole woof should have ate her up, huh?"

A sleepy voice from the far bed said, "Tell it again, T'oy?"

"Nope," said Kate, sitting up. "Prayers now. Can you say them, Torrey? I'll go tell Granny we're off."

It had been a long time since Torrey had said prayers at bedtime, her own or anybody else's. But the words came back. "Now I lay me down to sleep," and the children filled in when she faltered.

"Now the God Blesses," said the deep voice from the middle bed.

"You'll have to help me out," said Torrey. They called down blessings on everybody, including the two dogs and the cat.

"Now you have to kiss us."

Torrey stooped over each bed in turn, her neck almost jerked off by the hugs. They were sweet, she thought, sweet and full of a terrible vitality.

45

"You know what?" said the small boy in the middle bed. "You are a real good storyteller. I could just see that ole woof!"

Torrey squeezed him tight, her heart warmed by his words, before she tiptoed out.

"I wanna drink of water," called a small voice behind her.

"Oh, no, you don't," said Kate. "You had your chance to get a drink when you washed up."

"But I'm firsty!"

"Tell it to the sandman," ordered Kate. She began gathering up her things.

"Can we just go off and leave them?" asked Torrey.

"Sure. Granny's here. They'll be sunk before we get the car started. Granny's a good baby sitter, but she can't cope with the bedding down. I nearly can't myself. I don't know how Nora does it, day in and day out, with two more and one of them Biddy."

"They're darling!" said Torrey.

"Sure are. I wouldn't mind a half a dozen of my own. You're darn lucky, Torrey; you're at least headed that way."

Torrey's heart constricted. But am I? she wondered. If I can't have Cleve, I don't want anybody. I want Cleve's children. Cleve's and mine. Oh, Cleve!

Kate snapped off the lights in the living room. As she came back into the hall, she caught sight of Torrey's face and pulled up short. "Tor! What's wrong?"

"Nothing," answered Torrey, her voice breaking. "Absolutely nothing!" Her mouth twisted. She turned blindly toward the door.

Kate gathered her into her arms. "I might have

46

known something was wrong when you turned up so quick. That old bag get you down? Where's Cleve?"

"He's gone. By now he's gone."

"Gone where?"

"To South America. To Chile. On a plane. For a year."

"Here's a piece of tissue. That dratted old cat. And where's your diamond, Tor?"

"I gave it to Miss Clevinger."

"Are you ever crazy! Cleve gave that to you. It wasn't hers, was it?"

"The ring doesn't matter. It doesn't, Kate, really. I've never felt comfortable with it. But Cleve—Oh, o-K-Katie!" Torrey's head dropped on Kate's shoulder, and her body shook with sick waves of misery.

"You poor baby!" Kate's big hand held Torrey's dark head tight against her shoulder. "Come on now. Look, want a coke? Some coffee? No? Well, let's go. We can talk on the way. I'll drive."

They hurtled through the starlit night, with the Peninsula towns lying like sparkling jewels against the hills. The dark waters of the bay brooded on their right as they rattled along the freeway.

Torrey talked, and Kate listened. "Miss Cluney Mary is cruel and mean, and I hate her," finished Torrey. "I hate her with all my heart and soul."

"That's a mortal sin," commented Kate. "It'll rest heavy on your heart."

Torrey slid down on the seat with her head resting on the back of it. She felt spent. As they started up the bridge ramp, she burst out again. "The worst of it is, Kate, I've lost my degree in the shuffle. I shouldn't have let anything interfere with that.

I've worked for it for five years. The family's finances have been stretched to the breaking point. Then I didn't have the moral courage to see it through. It doesn't seem possible I could have been such a idiot!"

"You can't go to Doc Jordan?"

"How can I? 'Please, Dr. Jordan, I thought I was going to marry Cleve Macklin and wouldn't need a degree. Now I'm not, and I do. I haven't done the required work, but can't you just overlook that?'"

They drove through the Treasure Island tunnel, with the lights of the oncoming cars stabbing at them, splintering against the sides of the tunnel, turning them into shimmering, watered silk.

As the stream of cars flowed down the bridge, Torrey closed her eyes. When she heard a plane above the bridge, her head jerked up. But it was a small plane headed east. Cleve's must have gone long since. Somewhere in the soft night a high silver plane, winking and blinking among the stars, carried an excited boy off on a great adventure. With him went Torrey Thorne's heart and all the high hopes she and he had had together.

Torrey shut her mind to the future ahead of her. She thought of the sound of Cleve's voice, his brief kisses, the fun they had had with the square dancers.

"Remember, Muddy Face, I love you." She could hear his last words and the kiss he sent singing over the wires. She hugged the silly, barren words to her.

Something Dr. Jordan had said came back to her. "The most important thing to remember is that your own personality must shine through your words. Let your tones have warmth, kindliness, interest in your fellow beings." There was warmth in Cleve's last

48

words. Nobody could say words like that and not mean them.

As they turned into the boardinghouse driveway, Torrey turned to Kate. "Katie, I love Cleve and he loves me. I'm as sure of that as I'll ever be sure of anything. We'll just have to wait a little longer than we thought. It'll be easier for him than it's going to be for me. Right now, from here, it looks like a long, rough road. But I can wait. It's worth it."

When the fight begins within himself
A man's worth something

ROBERT BROWNING—MEN AND WOMEN

6

TORREY KEPT ON WITH HER CLASSES, although she
knew that without the credits for Storytelling,
she wouldn't be able to get her degree. She typed
up the Public Relations paper, giving it more time
now that she had no dates with Cleve. It sounded
better than she had thought. She put in hours of
hard study on the three exes coming up. I'll go down
fighting, she decided.

She was tempted to skip Dr. Jordan's class, but
pride wouldn't let her. At the end of the week, when
Dr. Jordan asked if someone else had a story, Torrey
raised her hand. He pursed his lips and teetered
on his small feet, glanced around the class at the
other hands, and finally nodded to Torrey.

With her heart pounding she walked up to the
head of the class. "This is an ancient Scottish myth,"
she heard herself saying, " 'How Spring Came to
Scotland.' "

Torrey put everything she had learned except
laughter into this story. It was a harsh story, full of

bitterness and woe, a story of storm and strife. Much of her own misery went into it.

She sat down to a burst of spontaneous applause. "That is one of the best stories we have had this year," commented Dr. Jordan, "told with vigor, fine picture-making, and a deep sense of doom. Too somber for young children, isn't it? If used with older children, there should be something else to lighten the mood." He made a mark in his little black book.

Was it enough? Would he let her by on the strength of it? Torrey dared to hope.

That afternoon she approached the lists with panic and hope struggling in her heart. When her name wasn't there, she felt a shock of anger against Dr. Jordan, followed by a shamed scorn for herself.

There was a final twist, an ultimate misery to be wrung dry. She gathered a handful of nickels and dimes and found the nearest phone box. In seconds she heard her mother's voice.

"Mom? This is Torrey. No, I'm all right."

Her mother's voice came back, happy to hear from her, a little puzzled. "Dad and Dave and I are planning to come up to see you get your degree. We'll bring you home for a rest. You must be worn out."

"You won't need to come, Mom. I'm not going to make it."

"What's that? Shake your phone, Torrey. I can't hear you very well."

"I said"—her voice broke. Then she took a deep breath. "Can you hear me now, Mom?"

"Yes, that's better."

"I'm not going to get my degree. I needed every

single credit to make it. I didn't pass in Storytelling."

"But, Torrey, I thought you were doing so well in that!"

"I know. But I couldn't—didn't—get all the work done. I didn't make it."

There was a moment's silence at the other end of the line. And then: "You must be tired out, Torrey. Come on home. Have you money enough?"

"I'll drive down."

"What about all your things?"

"I haven't got that far yet, Mom. I called you as soon as I knew."

This wasn't quite true. Torrey had known for several days that she wouldn't make it. But there had been a little sneaking hope that Dr. Jordan would relent at the last minute—on the basis of— well, of his enthusiasm for her first stories. But he had certain requirements for his course, and Torrey knew that she hadn't met them. She hadn't expected to see her name on that list. She would have been stunned with surprise if she had found it there. But until she knew for sure, she hadn't called Mom.

"It'll be good to have you home," Mom said. "It's been a long time."

When Torrey hung up, she rested her forehead against the round mouthpiece of the telephone for a moment. She hadn't been home for more than two months—not since before the Wolf Ridge Square Dance where she had met Cleve Macklin. Why hadn't she? Because every week end had been filled with Cleve, filled to the very brim with picnics at the beach, plays in the city, dances at Wolf Ridge, pizza at Lupo's. When she should have been taking Cleve home to see if he liked her people and they liked him. When she should have been learning stories so she had a degree in her fist right this minute to pay her folks back for five years of stretching to make a small ranch pay for an expensive college education.

Torrey wasn't sparing herself anything now that it was too late. But she was also realistic about it. I'd do it all over again, she was thinking, if Cleve were here—if Cleve were still here!

She studied hard that afternoon and evening and felt satisfied with the blue book she handed in at the end of the three-hour examination in the morning. As she walked out of the building, she came face to face with Dr. Jordan. She would have brushed on by, but he blocked her path.

"Good morning, Miss Thorne."

"Good morning," muttered Torrey, her face flushed.

Dr. Jordan stroked his pointed beard with nervous fingers. "No one regrets more than I do, Miss Thorne, that failing my course meant losing your degree." There seemed to be real concern in his voice.

"Except myself," said Torrey bitterly.

Dr. Jordan's lips pursed as he teetered on his small feet. "I still feel that you were my most promising student. I have talked with the Library School faculty. If you can get these few credits behind you, it will be possible to get your degree."

"Dr. Jordan!" Henrietta's mellow voice boomed out. "I want to thank you for your recommendations."

Torrey edged her way around them and made her escape. She finished up some tag ends. When she got back to the boardinghouse, Kate was there packing.

"Which will you have, Modom," asked Kate, "the curtains *or* the bedspreads? 'The time has come, the walrus said,' and 'I'll take the high road, and you'll take the low road'—Oh, the divil himself take my tongue! That wasn't the thing to say. Foot-in-her-mouth Kate, that's me."

Torrey laughed. "Low road is about it. Which do you want?"

"I'm going to be at Nora's all summer, going to summer school. Maybe Biddy'd feel better about my moving in with her if I brought those cute bed-spreads to doll up her room."

"Take the curtains too, Kate. They go together."

"Okay. I'll buy them from you, she said with an expansive gesture that didn't mean a thing on ac-count of I'm stony. But I can pay you out of my first salary, Simon Legree."

"It's a deal. Heard from Placement?"

Kate's face clouded over. "I got a school in Belve-dere."

"Wow! Maybe you can live on the lagoon and sail a boat."

"Sure, and join the Yacht Club and buy a mink stole." Kate rocked back on her heels.

"But Marin County is tops."

"Not in my book. I put it in because you had to list more than one choice. I wanted the Peninsula so I could be near Nora. I was going to take the little room off the garage. I'd like to be closer. With Bob gone, Nora needs a break. Five hellions—and one of them Biddy."

"You can go week ends."

"Sure. But you get involved where you are. And Biddy needs somebody to take her down and build her up. Biddy gets by with murder."

Torrey began stripping her bed, folding the blankets and sheets.

"You know," said Kate, "it's funny. All my life I've wanted things I couldn't afford. I couldn't ski because I couldn't afford the skis. I couldn't golf because I couldn't afford the fees. I couldn't ride during the summers because I couldn't afford a horse. Now I'm going to be on my own, with good hard cash coming in, and all I can think of is now I'll have enough money to get Biddy a new formal."

Torrey brought out a suitcase and opened it on the bed. "Maybe you do too much for Biddy and not enough for Kate."

"Could be. But, Tor, she's just where I was a few years back. She's a quivering bundle of wants."

"Aren't we all? Didn't hurt you not to have anything. Made you into quite a gal."

"But it seared my soul not to have *anything*. Biddy's pretty, devastating. Nora can't keep up with her. Nora has to work like fury, just to keep everybody in shoes."

"And Grandma," added Torrey.

"Nope. Granny pays her way. She has a little dab of pension and she blows the whole works on the family."

That's where Kate gets it, thought Torrey. All give and no take. She was going to miss Kate.

Torrey carried the suitcase down to her car. Then she and Kate made dozens of trips with boxes and bags, a lamp, the Chinese scroll Cleve had bought her in Chinatown. The trunk and the back seat were piled high, with dresses and suits hung from the hooks above the side windows.

As Kate stacked the last armload of books on the front seat, she asked, "You going to sit on the top of this moving van?"

"I'll sit small." Torrey pressed her palms against her temples. "You forget how much junk you accumulate."

"So long, Tor. Come up to Nora's whenever you can. And let me know how things go."

Torrey started the car and straightened the wheels. "'Bye, Katie. You've been wonderful—" Later, as she climbed the hills, she could see the college town spread out beneath a film of summer smog. She was going to miss Kate. She was going to miss college. Above all else, she was going to miss Cleve.

How should I your true love know
From another one?

WILLIAM SHAKESPEARE
—OPHELIA'S SONG FROM HAMLET

7

Two HOURS LATER, hot and tired, Torrey drove into the gate of the Thorne ranch. She was thankful that the car had made it.

Her mother hugged her tight. "So good to have you home," she said. "Come on in and have a bite of lunch before you unpack."

"Where's Dad?"

"He's gone to town."

"Dave?"

"Around somewhere. He'll be in for a bit when he gets hungry. They were irrigating all night. Don't know why we always have to take our water at night."

Mrs. Thorne was shorter than Torrey, plump and brown like a Valley quail. Her eyes were warm and brown like Torrey's, but her hair was gray, and her skin looked leathery beside the peach bloom of Torrey's face.

The two of them walked into the house, the

screen door easing shut behind them. It was good to be home, thought Torrey. The familiar smell of the Thorne house swept over her. It didn't smell old, like the Clevinger house. It had a fresh, clean smell, a sort of new-mown-hay smell, thought Torrey. That was silly, she thought. Except for a few acres of alfalfa, the Thornes didn't raise hay. Maybe it was grape blossoms. Something clean and sweet.

The table in the bay window of the kitchen was set with ivy-patterned place mats. The glasses were of blue Mexican glass. In the center of the table there was a blue bowl with yellow marigolds.

"It's good to be home again," said Torrey.

With quick, deft movements Mrs. Thorne put a fruit salad in front of her daughter, and a tall glass of iced tea. "Now," she said, sitting down across the table from Torrey, "what's all this about not getting through?"

Torrey squeezed a lemon wedge into her glass and dropped it in. She looked out into the shade of the grape arbor. Then she met her mother's eyes. "I didn't make it. I had to make a B average. Dr. Jordan had certain requirements. I didn't get them done. That's all."

Mom stirred restlessly. "Dad's going to want more than that. I haven't told him you didn't make it."

"I haven't any excuse, Mom. I met a man. I—I fell in love with him. His name is Cleve. Clevinger Macklin. I got so wound up with dates and things, I didn't get the work done in the storytelling class."

"Torrey! Who is he? Where did you meet him? When will he be coming here to see us? Is he also in love with you?" The questions came tumbling out.

58

Torrey pushed her salad back. "I'm not hungry, Mom. I met him at a square dance at Wolf Ridge. He's gone. He's gone to South America. He's in love with me. I know it. We're engaged."

"Then why did he go off to South America?"

Torrey wanted to shout at her, Because a beastly old woman wanted him to. But she curbed her resentment. "He has a chance to get a real start. He's just passed his Bar examinations. He's to be a lawyer for some people down there. He says he'll send for me as soon as things are settled."

"You mean you plan to go down to South America? To marry him down there?" When Torrey nodded, she said, "Dad's not going to like this."

"Well, that's the way it is."

"I wish you'd brought him home first. This sounds serious, Torrey. We should know something about him."

"I wish I had. But it all happened so fast. All I can say is that I love him and he loves me, and I'll go if—when—he sends for me."

Torrey's brother Dave came into the kitchen. He looked a little like her, but his eyes were hazel. He was stocky, with unruly brown hair, big feet, and a broad grin.

"Hi, Sis. Anything to eat, Mom?"

"Bacon and beans and salad."

"Skip the grass. I'll make a Dagwood outta the beans and rolls."

"It's revolting," said Torrey, watching him plaster beans and catsup on half a roll.

"Mom says you didn't get through. We were all set to come up and see you. What's the dope?"

59

"I didn't make it." She was stirring her tea again, watching the lemon peel turn and whirl.

"Torrey's engaged, Dave," said Mom.

"No kiddin'? Who? What? Why? Etcetera. Should be good to get you so confused, after all these years of colossal struggle to dig up the money."

The phone rang and Mrs. Thorne went off to answer it.

Dave sank his big white teeth in the dripping sandwich. "Dad will sure have a catfit. What you going to do now? Or do you expect him to come through for another six months?"

Torrey was surprised at the deep undercurrent of resentment in his voice. "I don't expect anything."

"Well, that's something. I'm the only guy in the county without a hot rod. For why? Because all the spare cash went into this extra year for you. And you got the car. The very car I'd picked for a hot rod."

Dave threw his head back and tossed the last of his iced tea down his throat. His mobile young face changed as he watched his sister put her hands palm down on the table in a little sick gesture of defeat.

"Where is this goof that's got you all tangled up? When's he coming down here so's I can size him up and decide if he's good enough for us. If he's after your money, my girl—"

Torrey failed to rise to this. "He's gone," she said, bleakly.

"Gone where?"

"South America."

"Well, how do you like that! Jilted!"

"I have *not* been jilted!" shouted Torrey. She half

rose from the table as her mother came into the kitchen.

"That was Ruth Rector," said Mom. "The PEO's are having a pot-luck tomorrow night, out at Hardy's. When she heard you were home, Torrey, she said to bring you, as well as Dad and Dave. She was surprised when I told her you were here, because I told her just yesterday we wouldn't be at the pot-luck because we were all going up to see you get your degree. I just told her you didn't make it. I didn't know what else to say."

Torrey flushed. "I wouldn't dream of going," she said angrily, crumpling up her paper napkin.

"What you going to do?" demanded Dave. "Sit around here with your head in a hole like an ostrich?"

A pick-up drove past the kitchen window and under the arbor.

"Here's Dad now." Mom's voice was a little tense.

"I'll go help him unload." Dave went out singing, "'Y' load sixteen tons, an' what d'y' get—'"

"He'll want iced tea." Mom peered into the frosty pitcher.

Torrey carried her dishes to the sink, rinsed them, and stacked them in the dishwasher. She resisted the impulse to run upstairs and shut herself into her room, as she used to do when she was in high school and things got too difficult for her in the family circle. She couldn't run away from this.

It had been hard enough talking to Mom and Dave. Her dad was something else. It wasn't only his quick flashes of temper. Torrey knew that her father's opinion mattered more to her than Dave's or even her mother's. She couldn't bear to let him know that she had failed him.

Through the kitchen window she watched him climb out of the pick-up. Why, he looks old, she thought. Beside Dave's young strength Dad seemed gangling and a little stooped. He was a long, thin man with a gaunt face and deep-sunk, dark eyes. In grammar school Torrey had thought of him as looking like Abe Lincoln. In high school she had been ashamed of his homely face and deliberate ways and the wrinkles in his sunbrowned neck above collars that always seemed a little bit too big. In college she knew his face for what it was, the patient face of a hard-working man, with wrinkles of kindliness and wry humor about his mouth, of worry and strain about his eyes. Where her mother had spread and broadened with the years, her father had thinned and then grown stooped.

"Mom has some iced tea for you, Dad." Torrey could hear Dave. "I'll take the stuff to the barn and unload."

Dan Thorne took off his battered straw hat and wiped his forehead with the back of his hand as he came onto the back porch. "Hot as blazes in town. Good to have Dave here to help unload. I'm getting too old to buck sacks." He gave a rueful little laugh as he put his hand on Mom's plump shoulder for a moment. "Why, Torrey!"

Torrey stood by the sink for a long moment. Then she ran across the room and was in the warm circle of her father's arms. "Daddy!" she said like a small girl. "Oh, Daddy!"

"Thought you were up at college. We were coming up tomorrow for the big doings."

"Sit down here, Dan," said Mom. "Had your lunch?"

"I had a bite in town. Tried that new Chinese place. All pork and glue."

"Sit here, Torrey. More iced tea?"

Mom put out another glass, pushed across the sugar bowl and lemon.

Dad poured himself a glassful, put in four teaspoons of sugar, squeezed in half a lemon, and dropped the lemon in the glass. Torrey watched him stir it round and round.

"How d'you happen to come home today?" Her father tipped up his glass and Torrey watched him as he drank. "Lord, that's good! Best thirst-quencher in the whole world. I don't know what your mother does to it. The brew they give you in town tastes like quinine." He turned to Torrey.

Torrey took a deep breath. "I came home because I didn't make my grades. I didn't get through. I won't be getting my degree."

Dad put his glass down on the table. He looked at her from under his jutting eyebrows. "How'd that happen? Thought you were all set."

"I was." It was hard for Torrey to find the right words. "But I met Cleve."

"Cleve?"

"Cleve Macklin. He's a boy—a man I met at Wolf Ridge. I—we—we're engaged. I'm going to marry him." She said it over to be sure, to make it sound certain in her own ears. "I'm going to marry Cleve."

"Where is this Cleve?"

"He's in South America. Chile."

"Let's get this straight." He took another long gulp of tea. "You got engaged to some chap in

South America and you didn't finish up at college?"

"No, Daddy. Cleve was here. He left for South America three days ago. He has a job down there."

"How long you been engaged to this—Cleve?"

"Since—" she had to stop and think. "Since last Saturday."

"That's the end of the term. How come you didn't finish your school work?"

Well, there it was. How could she explain? How could she make anyone else know the dearness of Cleve, the joy of going out with him night after night, the thrill of week-end dates full of gay surprises, the excitement over the big diamond, the bitter pill of that last phone call, and the sick feeling as she thought of Miss Cluney Mary? With the handle of a spoon Torrey was tracing the ivy-leaf pattern on the place mat before her.

Mom sat down beside her. "Pour me a glass of tea, Dan. Start at the beginning, Torrey, so's we'll understand a little better. You met Cleve at a dance. At whose home?"

"It was at Wolf Ridge. It's a kind of country club. People go there for the folk dancing. Kate and I went one night. Cleve was there."

"Who was the chaperone?" asked Mom.

"Chaperone?"

"Wasn't there a hostess or someone? Who introduced you?"

"Why, nobody. Anybody can folk-dance. You dance together and then you know people. Cleve called me the next day."

Mom was frowning. "I've often thought that the European system of arranged marriages had its points," she commented. "Did you ever meet his family? Where does he live?"

"He doesn't have a family. He was raised by his godmother. She's Miss Cluney Mary Clevinger and she lives down the Peninsula at Marysdale. He'd been staying at the Alpha Delt house until he passed his Bar examinations."

"Did you ever meet this Miss Clevinger?" asked Mom.

Torrey shut her eyes for a second as a wave of feeling poured through her. The kitchen seemed unbearably hot. "Yes. I was there for dinner."

Mom settled back, a little happier. "Does she approve of this engagement?" she asked.

Torrey lowered her eyes again to the ivy pattern. She wanted to say, She not only doesn't approve, she's busted it up. But she took herself in hand. "No," she answered, "she doesn't."

Mom bridled. "And why not?"

But Dad came back to another question. "I still don't see why you failed to pass. Even supposing you might get engaged to this boy at the last minute, didn't getting through seem important enough? It took some doing to scrape up the cash here at home."

Torrey winced. She looked up at him with sorry eyes. "I know." Her voice was almost a whisper.

His anger flared. "You know! What do you know? Looks like you don't know much. You don't know what it means to meet mortgages and crop loans and pay taxes and eat and save out money for board and room and clothes and tuition and—"

"Now, Dan, wait a minute. Torrey says she is going off to South America to marry this boy."

"You're *what*?"

Torrey sat up straighter. She set her jaw and looked her father in the eye. "As soon as Cleve sends for me I'm going down there to marry him."

She saw the vein in his temple swell and pulse. He banged the table so hard the glasses bounced, but his voice was controlled. "How long have you known this young man?"

"I—since—since some time in April."

"Less'n two months. You've met this godmother of his how many times?"

"Once."

"Once. And she doesn't approve of this engagement, that it?"

"That's right."

"Of course she doesn't. We don't either. Silliest thing I ever heard of. You get swept off your feet by a boy after a few weeks, so far off you lose sight of a degree that would have given you a decent job and repaid us for the long grind of getting you through college. Now he's cut and run to South America, and you propose to follow him. On what? On foot?"

Torrey hadn't thought of where the money would come from to get to South America.

"You'd have to have clothes too, Torrey," Mom pointed out. "Or do you expect to go empty-handed?"

Dad rose to his feet. "Looks like you better stay here a while and give your mother a hand. That'll give you a chance to learn how to look out for a man before you go off half-cocked, chasing after a boy you hardly know, the other end of the world."

"I'll earn the money!" Torrey's voice was stubborn.

"Not a bad idea," her father said drily, "but it would have been a heap easier if you had earned the degree first."

8

TORREY CARRIED THE THINGS from the car up to her
room. It was blazing hot. The heat beat down on
the eaves, turning the small room into an oven. The
walls were hot to touch and there was no air stirring the crisscrossed nylon curtains. The room had
looked bare at first. Now it looked hopelessly clut-
tered, a confusion of books and clothes, papers and
boxes, the welter of programs and pictures. She
picked up a small snapshot, and there was Cleve.
Less than a week ago? Could so much have happened in so short a time?

They were in bathing suits, sitting on a driftwood
log at Half Moon Bay, their feet buried in the sand.
A single beach towel bound their shoulders together. They were laughing like happy maniacs at Katie,
the picture-taker. It didn't matter. All that mattered
was that they had been deliriously happy, bare arm
against bare shoulder, the sound of wind and surf
and laughter in their ears.

In the picture Torrey was holding her left hand

out self-consciously to show the shining diamond on her ring finger.

Had Cleve been restless even then? Fretting and fuming under all that laughter? Just marking time with a pretty girl until he could get on with the business of a career? Stealing her heart and mind away from the business of her own degree, her own career? Why, then, had he given her the ring?

I wish I hadn't let that woman have it, Torrey thought. The ring was a symbol, something tangible between herself and Cleve, a bridge, of sorts, to span the miles that separated them. The ring was something that might have held conviction for her family. It would have been a symbol for them too. Without it they had only her word for the earnestness of Cleve's love for her. They considered her a moon-struck girl. Dave said she had been jilted. Had she been?

As she stood there in the clutter of her room, Torrey was hearing Miss Cluney Mary's voice: "Would you prefer to let him write you for that freedom of choice—and the ring?" No. It was better to have given up the ring. But it should have gone back to Cleve, not to Cluney Mary Clevinger.

I've done nothing but make mistakes, Torrey was thinking. She looked down at the laughing faces in the picture. Everything I've done was a mistake— except loving Cleve. She felt suddenly bone tired, exhausted, drained of energy.

She turned blindly and pushed through the books and suitcases to the bed. She swept up the clothes and hangers and dumped them on a chair. She stretched out on the patchwork quilt that served as a counterpane. Behind her were a series of sleepless nights, of tense and worried days. She wished she could cry. Instead she fell sound asleep.

When she awoke it was late in the afternoon. Someone, Mom probably, had come in and put a light cotton blanket over her. It was cooler. A slight breeze stirred the curtains.

She jumped up, washed her face and hands at the washbasin behind the Japanese screen in the corner, and ran wet fingers through her hair. Her cotton skirt was mussed, but she straightened her belt and ran downstairs to the kitchen.

Mom pulled a pan of rolls from the oven. "Oh, Torrey! Have a good sleep?"

"Wonderful. But I didn't mean to."

"You must have needed it."

"My room's a mess. I meant to get it done."

"I'll help you after supper. It'll be cooler. Pecan rolls, Torrey. You always said you liked them best. Last of the pecans until fall. I've had them in the freezer. Put ice in the tea, Torrey, and cut up some lemons."

For a while it was as though she had never been away. But during dinner Torrey realized she had been away a long time. "Where's Dave?" she asked as they sat down.

"Ruth Rector called to say she couldn't get her car started," answered Dad. "He drove over to see what's the matter."

"Dave should have been a mechanic," said Torrey, buttering a piping-hot pecan roll sticky with brown sugar and spices.

Dad frowned. "He would have made money, that's sure. Five times as much and double overtime. But Dave's like his mother. There's a loyal

"Well, I didn't know. She doesn't seem your type, somehow."

"What's my type? What's yours? This guy that lit out for Brazil soon's he finds you fell for him?"

There was an awkward pause at the table. Dave went on, pouring himself more iced tea. "Jen doesn't have a college education—that what you mean?"

"No," said Torrey unhappily, "it isn't that."

"She's okay," said Dave. "Teach Jennie how to make pecan rolls, Mom, and I'll marry her."

Mom chuckled. "Better see if she'll have you first."

"I'll ask her when I get around to it," said Dave. "I'm the best catch in the county."

"Says hoot?" scoffed Torrey.

Mom came upstairs with her after the dishes were done. "Tell me where you want things and we'll do it in half the time."

They worked quickly and efficiently. Mom hung the clothes in the closet while Torrey emptied suitcases and put things away in drawers.

"Better get some of these woolens to the cleaner's, Torrey. From now on all you'll need is cottons."

Torrey stood in the middle of the room. She pushed her hair back from a damp forehead. "I won't be here very long, Mom. I'm going to get a job."

Mom's face fell. "Better get a rest, first. Why don't you get a job in Stockton? You could live at home. It would save you lots of money. And we'd love it."

Torrey picked up the snapshot of herself and Cleve at Half Moon Bay. "This is Cleve, Mom."

Mom took the picture over to the light. She looked at it a long time. "It's good of you, Torrey. And he looks real nice."

"Oh, he is, Mom. He's—he's dear!" What an understatement. But how could she explain to anyone what Cleve was like?

"Is that a diamond on your finger, Torrey?"

"Yes." Her voice was tense.

"Don't you wear it?"

"I don't have it any more."

"Did you give it back to him?" Mom's voice was full of concern. She knew heartbreak when she heard it.

"Miss Cluney Mary took it back."

"The godmother? Was it hers?"

Torrey stood at the dresser, her hands full of boxes, a brown scarf the color of her eyes hanging over her arm. "No, it wasn't. It was Cleve's. It was his mother's. It was intended for his engagement ring. He got it out of the bank and gave it to me that day at Half Moon. I only had it a few days."

"Then I don't see why—"

"It's hard to explain, Mom. She didn't like me."

"Any reason for that, Torrey?"

"No. I never saw her but that once. Maybe she wouldn't have liked anybody for Cleve. Like me, about Jennie and Dave. She arranged this trip to South America and fixed it so he'd have to go off that very day. I know she did. Then she had me to dinner. And after Cleve phoned from the airport—" Torrey stopped, choked with fury and frustration.

Mom looked down at the picture again. "And then—"

"She told me that perhaps Cleve would change. A year was a long time. He'd be meeting other girls, other women, in Chile. She said that the ring had been left in her care, just as he had. She said he

74

would outgrow the feeling he had for me, and did I want him to write for the ring when he did."

"So you gave it to her!" Mom's eyes were snapping. "She had no right—"

Torrey shrugged wearily. "The ring didn't matter, Mom."

"I think it matters a great deal. I think it was a mistake to give it to her."

"I suppose so." Torrey's voice was full of tears. "I seem to have made so many mistakes."

A second later she was in her mother's arms, crying out her heartbreak like a small girl.

Mom let her cry. "There, there, there," she crooned after a bit. "It's a wicked shame. If he really loves you, Torrey, he won't change. You'll see. A boy with a face like that, he'll be back for you. A year isn't so long."

"You don't know that woman. She's not going to let him."

"Then he isn't worth waiting for. If he can't stand up to her over this, Torrey, it's better to know it now. You'd find it a wretched business being married to a man under the thumb of another woman."

After breakfast in the morning Mom called Torrey upstairs. "Give me a hand with this chest, Torrey. It's yours now. We'll have to get busy filling it."

"But this is your hope chest, Mom."

"Just until you needed it." There was a light in Mom's eye. "A year's a powerful short time to get things together, but I've been nibbling away at it for some time."

They set the chest down at the foot of Torrey's

bed. Mom opened the lid and the pungent odor of cedar filled the room.

"I relined it with muslin that first year you brought that nice young man home for some skiing." She bustled off and came back with an armload of towels and pillow cases. "These may not suit your taste, Torrey. A lot of the wedding presents you get won't either. But they'll be a start."

Staring at the chest, Torrey felt an age-old urge in her heart. "Why," she said shakily, "it's like building a nest or something."

Mom laughed. "Of course it is. You'd miss half the fun if you didn't stitch some of your dreams into the things you take into your new home. And I would too. Everything I've made these last four years has been done with an eye on this chest."

"I have some finger towels Kate gave me for Christmas. Irish linen." Torrey's voice was dreamy.

"I'm going to put in that Madeira cloth Aunt Hattie sent me. It's too small for my table when there's company. I have almost enough crocheted squares for a counterpane, and patches for two quilts."

They could hear the phone ringing. "Torrey!" shouted Dave.

"Hi!" said Kate's warm voice over the phone. "The top of the mornin' to ye, Macushla."

"It's good to hear your voice, Kate!"

"Listen, Tor. There's a cablegram here for you. I came back for some things and I found it."

"Read it!"

There was the sound of tearing paper. "It's from Cleve. Still want me to read it?" Kate's voice was full of laughter.

"Of course, you goof! Think I could wait?"

" 'Darling,' it says first of all."

Torrey's grief and frustration and misery dropped from her like a heavy yoke after a long pull. "Go on!" she said.

" 'It's Chile down here without you. Love you Muddy Face. Letters follow. Cleve.' "

"Oh! Katie!"

"Feel better?"

"Do I!"

"Listen. I've a proposition for you. There's a job open at the Marysdale library for a part-time children's librarian. The pay's better than anything you can get down there. You could live at Nora's, in the little room out in the garage. There's a half bath—a hot and cold shower—and an electric hot plate. You can have it cheap. Then I could go off to Belvedere and not worry so much about Nora. Want it?"

Torrey's mind was in a whirl. The cable from Cleve. The chest waiting upstairs. It would take money to fill that chest, to buy the clothes she'd need.

"Yes," she answered recklessly. "Sure. What do I do?"

"I'll tell Nora. She knows the librarian. He'll write you."

Torrey went back up the stairs two at a time. She caught Mom about the waist and waltzed her around the room.

"Torrey! Stop it. What is it?"

"It's Cleve! It's Cleve! It's Cleve!" sang Torrey. "A cablegram. A cablegram from Chile. He's safe. He got there. He loves me."

"Well, that's a comfort."

"And I have a job. At Marysdale."

Mom's face fell. She sat down on the chest. "I was hoping you'd get one here. I kind of hoped we'd work on the chest together. Then I'd have you home for a few months."

Torrey didn't hear the yearning in her mother's voice. "I can earn money for the chest," she was saying breathlessly. "And buy clothes. Cleve says it's cold down there. It's their winter, isn't it? He says—"

"I must make a hot dish for tonight. Want to go, Torrey?"

"Where?"

"The pot-luck the Peosies are having out at Hardy's."

Torrey was thinking, Yesterday I wouldn't have gone. Yesterday I couldn't have faced them. Today I've heard from Cleve. I have a chance at a job. "I'd love to, Mom. You've given me a new lease on life with the hope chest."

"I suspect the cablegram helped."

Torrey laughed. "Yes, it did. Now I'll have to work like fury to get things ready to go to Marysdale." She gathered up the pile of soiled clothes and danced out of the room.

Mom sat still for a few minutes, her eyes on her worn fingers as they caressed the smooth brown wood of the hope chest. "You raise 'em to stand on their own feet," she said aloud, "and when they do, you just wish they wouldn't."

9

HER FATHER SAT AT THE LUNCH TABLE across from Torrey, glaring at her. "You mean to say you're going to take a half-time job and live away from home and stay in a garage?" His voice was raised over the roar of the cooler.

"It's a room next to the garage. It has a bath and a place to cook. Kate says I can have it cheap."

"How cheap?"

"Well, she didn't say."

He snorted. "And this job? What kind of a salary you going to get for a half-time job?"

"I don't know. Kate said it was more than I could get here."

"More than what? More than a half-time job here? More than a full-time job? More than what?"

"I don't know."

Dad blew his breath out in a puff of fury. "You don't know. That's all I've heard from you, young lady, since you came home. You didn't know enough to get your degree. And you don't know any better than to go traipsing off to a half-time job. You know what a half-time job means?"

"I don't—" Torrey stopped.

"No. You don't know. Well, nine times out of ten it means half-pay or less for a lot more than half-time work. You won't—"

"But Dan," Mom cut in, "why don't we wait and hear about it first."

"We've been hearing about it, right now. It doesn't add up to a grain of sense. She'll have to live up there on half-pay with expenses just as high as if she worked full time."

"Kate told her she could have this room cheap."

"She'll have to eat, won't she? You don't pick food off trees any more. Food costs money. If she lived here at home—"

"I don't *want* to live at home." As soon as the words were out Torrey wished she hadn't said them. She remembered a verse Dr. Jordan had read them in class: "Look out how you use proud words." She could see that she had hurt Mom, and angered her dad still further. Words were things you couldn't get back once they were spoken. As Carl Sandburg had said proud words wore hard boots and walked off proud.

Dan Thorne's face was red, and the pulse in his temple was jumping. "You'll live at home," he shouted, "and like it! Maybe we're not good enough for you. Too country!" He pushed away his plate and rose from the table, towering over Torrey. "I don't want another word out of you, young lady, about this half-baked job. You settle down here and give your mother a hand. Later you can look for a job in Stockton. They can use a college graduate in

80

banks, lots of places. Maybe you can learn a few country ways that will make you into a decent wife for a good American boy. Not some footloose foreigner south of the border."

Torrey was angry too. "Cleve isn't a footloose foreigner. He—"

"I don't want to hear anything further about this Cleve," he roared. "It's a cinch he isn't good enough for you or any other American girl." He banged his fist on the table. "Any man worth his salt would have come down here and talked things over. Looks to me like you've bought yourself a pig in a poke."

"I have not," answered Torrey. "I love Cleve, and he loves me."

Her father grunted. "You've been saying over and over, 'I don't know this and I don't know that.' What you don't know, either one of you, is the first thing about love. If he did he'd never have gone off and left his girl up here a week after they got engaged. And if you did"—he lifted his straw hat off a hook and bashed it down on his head—"you wouldn't have let him go!" He pulled open the kitchen door and kicked the screen door open. He slammed both doors behind him.

Torrey listened to the whirring of the cooler, tracing the pattern of the leaves on the plastic place mat with the tip of her fork. Her elation and excitement over the cablegram had given way to a deep depression. Maybe her dad was right. Maybe she and Cleve didn't know enough about love. Maybe Cleve didn't really love her if he could go off like this, leaving her at the mercy of a woman like Cluney Mary Clevinger, letting her face the criticism of her family, the anger of her father. Maybe . . .

Mom slid her work-worn hand over Torrey's. "I'd love to have you at home for a while, Torrey. You know that. But I don't feel as Dad does. I think Cleve loves you."

Mom's words warmed Torrey's heart. She felt badly about hurting her mother. She wished she felt differently about staying at home. But she wanted the chance to get out on her own. The thought of it frightened her. Could she make a go of it? She wasn't sure. But she knew she'd never be satisfied until she tried.

If Cleve changed his mind about her, she'd need to have a job. She knew it would be wiser to stay at home, to get a job close at hand. But she wanted to be independent, to try her own wings. She knew, too, that she couldn't stay home and listen to her father criticize Cleve.

Perhaps Cleve didn't love her enough. Perhaps he would never send for her. "Maybe Dad's right," she said unhappily.

"Well," said Mom, beginning to stack the dishes, "if he is, the sooner you find it out the better. It'll take a little time. In the meantime, if I loved him, I'd be willing to wait. I'd keep my faith in the man I loved until I had more reason for doubting than you have. Come along now and cut up some celery for me."

The next few days Torrey kept very busy. At the pot-luck supper she enjoyed her mother's friends. No one questioned her about her plans. They just seemed glad to see her again.

Jennie Rector was there too. She was a pretty girl with wide blue eyes, a too-curly permanent that spoiled the texture of her blonde hair, and an air of possessing Dave that Torrey found irritating. Torrey tried hard to like her because Dave did, but she found herself with nothing to say. She isn't good enough for Dave, she thought rebelliously. She's as contented and sure of herself as a prize cow.

There was plenty to do on the ranch for an extra pair of hands. Torrey was up feeding chickens and turkeys in the early morning, making fig jam, cooking, and cleaning, falling into bed by nine-thirty at night. She steadily refused Dave's invitations to go out with him and Jennie Rector.

Dave had worked over the car she had brought home, and he used it most of the time. "Runs like a Swiss watch," he told her. "Want to take it into town?"

"No, thanks." Torrey's voice sounded listless.

It worried Mom. When she mentioned it to Dad, he was irritated. "Leave her alone," he growled. "Time she earned her keep. She'll get over it."

He seldom spoke to Torrey, and she felt the burden of his disapproval. They had often disagreed over the years, being much alike, but she never remembered his anger holding as it held now. She haunted the mailbox, though Dad nearly always met the postman. She didn't know Cleve's address, and until she did, she couldn't write to him. Kate had mailed the cablegram and Torrey had read and re-read it until it was wearing thin along the creases.

The temperature crept steadily up over the hundred mark. It was muggy in the fields and orchards. The nights stayed warm, and the earth itself cracked under the merciless rays of the San Joaquin sun.

As the days went by and there was no word from

Cleve, Torrey was tempted to call Miss Cluney Mary long distance to ask for his address. But when she thought of the tall, brown figure smoothly moving up the stairs, and that last negligent gesture with the ring glittering on the bony hand, her pride wouldn't let her make the phone call.

She swept and dusted, baked and brewed, fed the stock and tried to keep cool in the Valley heat. Obediently she hemmed dish towels for the hope chest or helped Mom stitch quilt patches. She tried to share Mom's enthusiasm for the contents of the chest, but her heart ached with longing for more than the telegram from Cleve, for some reassurance that all these stitches were worth taking.

On Friday she had a letter from Kate that turned her world upside down. "Mr. Brock, the librarian," wrote Kate, "would like to see and talk with you. It's only a half-time job, but he says they can pay you one hundred and fifty dollars a month. He says as soon as you get those extra credits, they can place you in a full-time job. He suggests that you use the extra time to take a couple of courses at Library School. Nora says you can have the room for twenty dollars. Just having you here would give us both peace of mind, when Nora can't get home early, and Granny finds the children too much for her. Do come. Kate."

Torrey took the letter to her room and read it again. She wondered what food for one person would come to. Probably a lot. But surely her living expenses, with her present clothes to carry her along, wouldn't be over a hundred dollars, room included. That would leave fifty dollars a month for the hope chest.

Put it out of your mind, Torrey Thorne, she told herself. Settle down here and behave yourself. She knew that she could earn more than that close at home for a full-time job. But she couldn't ever get those lost credits over here.

She didn't want to stay at home. Her father might gradually get over his silent disapproval if she stayed, but she felt that he would never get over his criticism of Cleve. Dave was absorbed in Jennie Rector. The only one she would really hurt by going was Mom. She decided to talk it over with her.

Late that afternoon, with supper nearly ready, they sat sewing where they could get the air from the cooler without having it blow directly on them. The sound of the water dripping was a pleasant, cool sound, but the air was heavy with moisture.

"Mom."

"Yes. Torrey, tell me, do you like all these dark pieces in here?"

"Mom, I had a letter from Kate today."

"Good. Why don't you get her down here for a week end as soon as this hot spell breaks?"

"She says that the librarian at Marysdale wants to see me."

Mom put down her sewing, a worried frown between her eyes. "I hoped you'd forgotten about that."

"I can stay at Nora's for twenty dollars a month, and I can get a hundred and fifty dollars. Wouldn't that be enough so I could have something for the hope chest?"

"Not very much. You'd do better, with board and room free."

"But I can't do that. I'd want to pay for my board and room."

"We wouldn't expect it."

"Well, I would. Over there I'd be independent and—"

"Your dad would never forgive you."

"He hasn't anyway."

"He'll get over it." Mom held up the patch, squinting at it.

"I couldn't stay, knowing how he feels about Cleve."

Mom's blue eyes were pleading. "Wait a few more days, Torrey. Dad'll change. You'll see. I've never known him to hold a grudge."

But that night Dad boiled over. "Had a letter from that young man you've been telling us about?"

"No, I haven't."

"Darn tootin' you haven't. I've been watchin' that mailbox same as you have. I just wanted to be sure. Even by the slowest mail he should have sent a letter by now. Right?"

Torrey's eyes were wide with misery, her teeth clenched. She put her hands on either side of her plate as though to steady herself.

"Now Dan—" began Mom.

"It's high time this girl came to her senses. It's two weeks since that boy left her flat. Not even a good-bye. Just a phone call from the airport. What kind of a thing is that?"

"I've had a cablegram."

"When?"

"Kate phoned it to me, and then she mailed it."

"What did he say?" There was skepticism in his voice.

"He said it was cold down there. He said—he said some other things too." How could she tell him that Cleve had said, "Don't forget, Muddy Face, I love you." "And he said he'd write."

"But he hasn't, that it?"

Torrey didn't answer. She didn't want to quarrel with her father because it would hurt Mom.

Dan Thorne put his big hands on the table in much the same manner that Torrey had. "How we going to get it through this girl's head that she's wasting her time moonin' around over a no'count?"

Torrey stood up. She forgot about Mom. She forgot everything except that Dad was talking about Cleve. Her own voice was thick with anger. "How am I going to get you to realize that he isn't? If I never hear from him or see him again, I'll love Cleve Macklin until the day I die."

"Tosh!" sputtered Dad. "A lovesick girl full of play-acting."

Torrey wilted.

Dave grinned at her, and she made herself smile back at him. "How about a movie tonight, Torrey? I won't ask Jennie. Just you and me?"

"No, thanks. I have to pack."

"Pack!" Her father's voice cracked over the word as he stood up. The same tense stubbornness was in both of their faces.

"I'm going to try that half-time job on Monday," Torrey told him. "I'm going to Nora's now, tonight. Mind if I take your car into town to the bus station, Dave?"

"I'll drive you all the way to Nora's," he answered. "Too many changes between here and there. It's too hot to lug suitcases."

"You'll do no such thing!" thundered Dan Thorne.

"Keep your shirt on, Pa," said Dave. "I came of age years ago."

Dad glared at Torrey. "You! You'll stay right here where you belong."

Torrey couldn't trust herself to answer. She gave her mother's shoulder a little pat as she left the table. This would be hard on Mom. Torrey felt badly about that. I'm probably making another mistake, she thought miserably, but this is what I have to do.

An hour later she and Dave were driving north through the sticky heat, in the face of the setting sun.

When your heart is like to break,
And once again is like to break

OLD ENGLISH FOLKTALE
—THE BLACK BULL OF NORROWAY

10

TORREY HADN'T SEEN HER FATHER AGAIN. Mom had helped her pack and hugged her tight before she climbed into the car beside Dave.

"Write, Torrey, as often as you can?"

"I will, Mom. And don't worry. I'll be all right at Nora's."

Mom patted her own lips absently with tremulous fingers. She smiled resolutely. "Of course you will."

Torrey glanced at the kitchen door. But it remained obstinately shut. Her eyes swept up to the second story of the comfortable ranch house, where the nylon curtains hung limp against the windows of her room.

As the car ran down the drive between the oleanders and pomegranates, Torrey's heart was heavy with tears. This was more than good-bye to Mom. It was a leave-taking from all her childhood.

89

Behind her she was leaving all of her growing years, a warmth and security she had always known.

I'll never go back, she told herself, until I go with Cleve. There was no lift in the thought. She was leaving her family, but not for a haven with the man she loved. She didn't even have a job. Just the half-promise of a half-time job. Torrey was afraid, sorry and afraid, and full of an inner excitement. Half of her was torn with regret for what she was leaving behind her. But the rest of her was reaching out in fear and trembling to new horizons.

The ride was long and, for the most part, silent. They endured the heat and glare across the plains and up over the brown hills.

At the first breath of cool sea air, Dave began to bounce in the driver's seat. "Boy! That feels good! How you off for money, Sis?"

"I have about ten dollars."

"That won't buy peanuts. Here's twenty, and I'll send you some more next week, when I can get to the bank. You won't be paid for a while."

Torrey's voice was unhappy. "I can't take your money just like that, Dave."

"Bologna! You've got to have some cash. These super markets don't sell on time. You'll have to stock up with a lot of things to begin with. It'll take a lot more than a ten-spot."

Torrey took the money. "I'll pay it back out of my first check, Dave," she promised.

He waved the promise off grandly. "Wish you'd come home week ends, Torrey. For Mom's sake. She's not very happy about all this."

Torrey set her lips. "I won't come home now, Dave, until I can bring Cleve with me."

"You goin' down there to marry him?"

"I don't know." A week ago I'd have said yes, she thought. "I've thought a lot about it, Dave, waiting to hear from him. Dad's right, in a way. I don't know Cleve very well. It would be awful to make a mistake. I'd hate to get clear down to Chile—marriage is so—well, so final."

"Sure is. That's why I don't ask Jennie. You have to be dad-blamed sure. I'd like it better if you'd wait. A brother likes to know the guy he's going to let his sister marry."

Torrey smiled in the cool dusk. How young he sounded. And how dear. Not angry and full of fireworks, like Dad. Just earnest and full of responsibility.

"You'll like Cleve, Dave. He's a grand guy."

"I've known that all along. All the guys you've liked, I've liked too."

"I wish he'd write."

"Yeah. Know how to reach him?"

"No, I don't."

"Why don't you call his godmother?"

"I've thought of that. But she's not friendly, Dave. I think she'd resent it."

"What do you care? She doesn't like you anyway. You've nothing to lose. Give him another week and then ring her up. Where do we turn?"

Kate came out to meet them. "Come in, the both of you. I've Cokes in here, and all the family's still up. Come along. Granny's dying to meet you."

The house was a riot of sound and fury. The dogs were barking. The Siamese cat leaped up on a bookcase, staring at them with indifferent blue eyes. The three youngest children pounced on Torrey. "Tell us about the gunnisack."

"Leave be," shouted Kate. "Have ye no manners? Granny wants to meet them."

She led Torrey and Dave to a corner by the fire where a tiny, crinkled, and wrinkled old woman was sitting hunched over in a walnut rocker. Her gnarled hands rested on an Irish blackthorn stick. Her tiny feet in beaded slippers were perched on a carpet-covered hassock.

"This is Torrey and David Thorne, Granny," shouted Kate. "She's deaf," she added in a low voice.

"I hear what I choose," Granny said.

Kate laughed. "She lip-reads."

The old woman beamed upon them. "You're a bonny pair," she said. "But I thought Kate told me the man you had in mind, Torrey Thorne, was off and away."

"Dave's her brother," yelled Kate.

"That's better. Ye shouldn't be off with the old and on with the new in such a hurry. It ain't seemly."

"This is Biddy," Kate was saying.

Torrey looked at the sixteen-year-old girl sitting on the woodbox. Kate was right. Biddy was a beauty, with a flying color in her cheeks, violet eyes, and coal-black hair that hugged her heart-shaped face like the calyx of a flower.

Biddy rose from the woodbox with grace, spread her full skirt wide, and dropped a mocking curtsy, her eyes on Dave.

She's beautiful, thought Torrey, and sassy as all get out.

Torrey met ten-year-old Dennis, a quiet redhead

with glasses and red-brown freckles over most of his face.

"Nora's not home yet. I'm saving her supper. You sure you've eaten?"

"We had dinner at home early," answered Dave.

"That's a long time ago. Get some crackers and cheese from the safe, Biddy."

Biddy came in with a flourish. The cheese had been smacked uncut on a plate, a knife beside it. The crackers were still in the box.

"For shame on you, Biddy O'Shea!" cried Kate. "What gets into you that you can't do a thing properly?"

"I didn't want to miss anything," said Biddy, crinkling her blue eyes at Dave.

The little devil, thought Torrey. She's flirting with Dave. *Dave!* And barely out of the cradle.

He didn't seem to mind. He sat down beside Biddy on the woodbox, contentedly munching crackers and cheese.

Granny looked up at Torrey. "They tell me you're a storyteller, the children do. They told me the story you told them over and over. They do it pretty well, except I don't understand about the gunnysack."

Torrey laughed. "It's a gunniwolf, and your guess is as good as mine about a gunniwolf."

Granny nodded. "Everybody makes up his mind about a gunniwolf. But a gunnysack's a sack and no more. Do you know many stories?"

"Not very many. But I like to tell them. I enjoyed these children."

"Aye. They've learned to listen. It's a rare gift, d'ye know that?"

"I hadn't thought about it. I guess it is."

"I've told them stories since the day they were born. You can't begin too soon."

Kate interrupted them. "Come on out and see your room, Tor. Biddy and I have been fixing it up."

They all trooped out to the garage, leaving the old woman nodding in her chair. The room was small but clean and bright. There were slightly faded blue and maroon plaid curtains and a matching plaid bedspread on the single bed. There was a dark blue shag rug and blue pillows. Beside the bed was a lamp with a maroon shade. One door shut away a bath with a shower, another shut off a roomy closet. In the alcove between them was a tiny sink and a two-burner electric hot plate. A small desk, a battered overstuffed chair, and some bookcases completed the room.

"Think it's okay?" asked Kate.

"It's grand. I'll be very comfortable."

"What can you see out the windows?" asked Dave, trying to peer into the black night.

"Our back fence is the seminary's back fence," said Kate. "There are oaks out there and a playing field."

"It looks fine," said Dave. "I think you'll be all right out here, Sis."

"Wish you could stay here too, Dave," said Biddy batting her thick black eyelashes at him.

"Wouldn't mind," answered Dave as they walked back to the big house. "Wouldn't mind at all. Looks real snug. Glad I came along. Now I can tell Mom how nice it is."

"Oh!" Biddy pouted. "I thought you were going to say how nice *we* are!"

94

"Wouldn't want to perjure myself," answered Dave.

If Jennie doesn't watch out, thought Torrey, she'll lose Dave to a sixteen-year-old hellcat.

Nora Corrigan came in. Kate's sister was a tall, rangy woman with freckled hands and face. Her red hair was streaked with gray, but her eyes were as blue and lively as Kate's. There was a quiet strength to Nora that seemed to reach out and enfold her turbulent family.

She welcomed Torrey with warmth. "You're to feel as much at home in this house, Torrey, as you are out in your own room. We've told the youngsters they have to mind you, and you're to make it stick. They can do everything for themselves, even the little ones, but sometimes it takes some sharp persuasion to get them at it."

Dave left shortly after that, with Biddy riding down to El Camino Real with him.

"I need to get some white shoe polish," she explained blandly.

Nobody objected, least of all Dave, as he and Biddy drove off followed by shouts and laughter.

The next minute they were listening to Granny tell a story. Torrey forgot everything as she listened to the wild adventures of the wee red man, and watched Granny sharpen his knife and sharpen his knife with a bony old finger on her scraggly forearm.

"That's a gory story!" she told Granny after the youngsters had gone off to bed. "Legs cut off and people burned up and heads off and on again."

Granny chuckled. "It is that. It's why they like it. It's absurd, and there's laughter in it, and the

95

laughter keeps it sane. Children don't like stories too wishywashy. You mark my words, Torrey Thorne. If you want to tell stories, tell fierce ones. Tell stories the children can get their teeth into and remember. Dragons and flaming wheels and witches and hobgoblins. Ghosts too."

"I wish I could tell an Irish story like you do," said Torrey.

"Ho!" answered Granny. "I'd have to give you my father and my mother."

The old woman sank her chin on the gnarled hand that rested on the blackthorn stick. In a moment she was snoring gently.

Kate came back and sat down on a hassock in front of the fireplace. "What do you hear from Cleve?" she asked.

"Nothing."

"You mean—all this time and—nothing?"

"Just the cablegram."

"But he said he was writing."

"I haven't heard."

"Torrey!" Kate sat up. "Do you suppose he wrote to the boardinghouse, and they failed to forward it, like the cablegram?"

"He'd know by now I wasn't there. And I left a forwarding address."

"I just don't believe Cleve wouldn't write."

"I didn't think I could either. But he hasn't."

"I bet he has. Why, Tor, I never saw somebody so much in love with anybody as Cleve was with you. He couldn't—nobody could—fall out of love like that so soon."

Torrey shrugged. "I've tried to reason it out, Katie. I've tried to tell myself they've gone off some

96

where in Chile where he can't write. A long trip or something. I've tried to tell myself that Cleve's one of those people who just don't like to write. I've quarreled with my father over it. He thinks that Cleve's just plain no good."

"That's because he doesn't know Cleve. But I do. He's not like that. He'd get word to you some way. Have you written to him?"

"I can't. I don't know where he is. Santiago is a big city. I don't know the name of the man he went with."

Kate pulled the hairpins out of her mass of red hair and let it fall in a cloud over her shoulders. She stretched her long legs. "Tor, do you think—"

The door banged open and in came Biddy, a flashlight in her hand.

"Where's the polish?" asked Nora.

"Everything's shut."

"The market isn't."

"I didn't come that way."

Nora shrugged. "Well, you can't wear those white shoes to church unless you whiten them."

"I'll wear my red sandals. Dave gave me this flashlight, Torrey, and said to give it to you. But I wish I could keep it, on account of because it's his, and because he put it into my own lily white hands with his very own dirty paws."

"Keep it for now," said Torrey. "I'll ask for it if I need it."

Biddy stood by the fire, smiling a little secret smile, the flashlight against her flushed cheek. "How old is Dave?" she asked.

"He's twenty."

"I thought boys had to be in the service by then."

"He got deferred because of the ranch. But he says he is going the next time."

"Why?"

"He wants to be like the rest, I guess."

"He'll be dreamy in a uniform. He'll make a wonderful soldier." Biddy sighed and rolled her eyes.

"I think he plans to be a sailor."

"Sailors look divine in those cute tight pants."

"Aren't you a little young for Dave?" asked Kate.

"Don't be silly, Kathleen. I'm sixteen, and sixteen is almost seventeen."

"Not when your birthday was last month."

"Don't be so literal. I think Dave is simply sharp. And," she added, her eyes on the glowing coals, "I think—I'm almost sure—almost—he thinks I am too."

"He probably already has a girl," said Kate brutally.

"Has he?" Biddy demanded of Torrey. "Torrey, has he?"

Torrey was about to say yes he has, but I don't think she's good enough for him. Don't say it, she told herself. Don't give this nitwit a weapon like that. Jennie's far better for Dave than this little—this *child*.

"Has he?" Biddy's voice was urgent.

"Sure," answered Torrey easily. "Everybody always has somebody."

"Is it serious?" Biddy wanted to know.

"I don't know," Torrey answered honestly. She was hearing Dave's voice. "You have to be dad-blamed sure."

"That's all right then," said Biddy, pulling off her sweater and draping it over her shoulders. She paraded down the room, followed by the padding boxers. She swung her arms up like a ballet dancer, digging one heel of her flats into the instep of the other. "I'll knock her right out of his head."

"She's there and you're here," Kate pointed out.

"I can write, can't I?" Biddy turned slowly and gracefully on her toes. She came down to earth slowly, bunching her skirt in the circle of her arms. "If you're in love with somebody—*really* in love—you don't let anything—not *anything*—stand in the way."

There was a stricken silence in the room. Torrey stood up. "If you don't mind," she said in a tired voice, "I'll go to bed."

And dar'st thou, then
To beard the lion in his den . . . ?

11

THE NEXT MORNING Biddy was sitting cross-legged on the unmade bed in Torrey's room filing her fingernails. "Torrey, do you think chivalry is dead?"

"No. Times have changed. Women in America—"

"But boys at our school just laugh if you stumble and drop things. They don't tip their hats because they don't ever wear any. They never give you a seat in a bus, and they'd die before they'd help you into a car—all but Dave."

"Dave's older."

Biddy went on. "My father must have been like that. Very handsome and debonair. Debonair means sophisticated, Torrey, and suave, and a lot of things. He left me a great gift."

Torrey was a little startled. She had thought Bob was in the offing someplace.

"He bequeathed me his good looks," said Biddy. "He gave me a face that could launch a thousand ships."

100

"Is your father—?"

"He's dead." Biddy's voice was cheerful. "He died before Dennis was born. It seems dreadfully sad to come into the world after your parents are dead, doesn't it? It marked Dennis. I don't remember our father, but I have his picture. He looks like me and he was terribly, terribly handsome. I don't see how Nora could marry anybody like Bob after that, do you?"

"I don't know Bob," said Torrey, her voice disapproving.

"He's okay, I guess. Dennis thinks the world of him. He's a writer but he never sells anything. He's in Mexico getting dope for a new book. He never sends us any money, so I guess he's in the same old rut. I think a man should stay home and take care of his family, don't you? Wouldn't you think he'd rather do an honest day's work, instead of leaving it all for Nora to do?"

Torrey laid the books she was unpacking on the top of the bookcase. "I don't think you should discuss things like that outside your own family, Biddy."

Biddy made a face. "Don't be stuffy. You're part of the family. It's one of the penalties you pay for the privilege of bossing us. And I should be able to tell you my troubles. It's one of the prime needs of teen-agers. A writer—I'm going to be a writer— like Bob, only I'm going to sell everything—has to analyze people. It isn't gossip. I analyze people all the time. I analyzed you right away."

Torrey laughed. "Jump up now. I need to analyze this bed and get it made."

"I'll help."

Torrey could have made the bed twice over by the time it took Biddy to do her half. Biddy talked the whole time while Torrey half listened.

She was worried about a number of things. Sheets and blankets, towels and washcloths. Surely all that didn't come under twenty dollars rent? It would mean a large outlay. The thirty dollars she had wouldn't go anywhere if she had to buy sheets and pots and pans.

Out of the middle of her thoughts she heard Biddy's voice: "—because I'm a genius."

"You sure?"

"Yep. I have an IQ of one hundred and sixty. I heard the teachers talking about it. What's a genius?"

"Anybody with an IQ of one hundred and sixty," answered Torrey, grinning.

"That's right."

"Anybody with an IQ of one hundred and sixty ought to be able to miter a sheet better than that, Biddy O'Shea."

Biddy jerked the sheet out and started over. "You don't pay much attention to what I'm saying, Torrey."

"I'm thinking about sheets and things and wondering if I'll have enough to get my own until I get paid." Goodness, she thought, I don't even have a job.

"Mom's got tons."

"She needs tons for all those beds. Washing in this house must be something."

"Yes, it is. Mom says if we just didn't have to eat and sleep she could manage."

102

"Shouldn't you be over there helping her?"

Biddy pouted. "I suppose so. She doesn't know where I am. She thinks I'm doing the dishes."

"Come on, we'll both do them."

"Are you ever crazy. You don't have to."

"If I'm going to use Nora's sheets and things, it's the least I can do."

Torrey was interested to see how Nora managed to tuck eight people into a three-bedroom house. Nora and Granny had a small room together. Kate was in one twin bed and Biddy in the other in a pleasant room overlooking the seminary. Dennis had a couch in the glass-enclosed lanai, and the three children slept in the master bedroom. There were four beds in there packed close together.

"For company," explained Biddy. "I move in here depending on whether they're the same sex or married. If they aren't married, Dennis moves out to your room. Once Dennis and I slept on the lawn, but we got up early and came inside, so the neighbors wouldn't see us. I think it's kind of poverty-stricken to sleep on your lawn, don't you?"

"Sounds like fun," answered Torrey.

"Stop your chatter, Biddy, and make Granny's bed," scolded Kate. "Let's call the boardinghouse, Tor, and ask if there's any mail over there. Cleve's letters have to be somewhere."

When there was no mail Torrey shrugged to hide her disappointment. "Guess I'll have to come to my senses, as my dad said."

"It doesn't make sense," said Kate frowning. "Cleve still thinks you have his ring. He doesn't know about

103

Miss Cluney Mary—" Kate's eyes flew open. "That's where your letters are!"

"Mary who?" asked Biddy.

"I suppose I could phone." Torrey's voice was uncertain.

"I wouldn't," said Kate. "I'd go right up there and get them. If she's holding Cleve's letters deliberately—"

"She doesn't know where I am. She didn't ask where I lived."

"I bet he told her where you were. If he sent the letters to her, he told her."

"*Who* is Loony Mary?" demanded Biddy again.

"Miss Cluney Mary Clevinger. She's Torrey's fiancé's godmother."

"*The* Clevinger?"

"Yes. She doesn't want Cleve to marry Torrey. She took Torrey's ring, and now we think she's holding Cleve's letters."

"We don't know for sure," said Torrey.

"How frightfully exciting," breathed Biddy. "It's like a Victorian romance. It's like locking people in their room on bread and water. It's like the Barretts of Wimpole Street. You know, the Oedipus complex or something. Can I go with you, Torrey, to get the letters? Please! Nothing romantic or exciting ever happens around here. What will you do if she won't give them to you? Suppose she just says there weren't any? What could you do? You can't exactly bash her on the head and hunt for them. Maybe she's burned them. You'd have to sift the ashes. Maybe she's torn them into little bits and flushed them down—"

104

"Oh, shut up, Biddy!" said Kate. "Your tongue is hinged at both ends."

"I'd never get up the courage to face her again," muttered Torrey.

"Look!" offered Biddy. "I'll go."

"And suppose she doesn't have any letters," said Torrey. "I couldn't bear to let her know I haven't heard from Cleve."

"That's false pride," said Biddy, bouncing up and down on the last bed. "I'll phone. She won't know my voice. And I'll say, 'This is a friend of Cleve's, Miss Cluney Mary Clevinger, and he wrote me to say that he has sent letters to Miss Torrey Thorne and he has had no word from her.' No, let's see. 'He tells me he sent the letters to *you*, Miss Clevinger, and *you*—'"

"Oh, Biddy, do hush. What do you think, Torrey?"

Torrey didn't know what to think. With all her heart she wanted to hear from Cleve. But how could she be sure he had sent letters to Miss Cluney Mary? How could she put her pride in her pocket and ask?

"Let's wait," she decided. "When Cleve doesn't hear from me, he'll do something about it. He'll know I haven't heard, and he'll do something."

"Oh, gee," said Biddy. "So we wait. Here we have some real drama, and you two old fogies want to *wait!*"

"You'll wait too, Biddy O'Shea, and no nonsense."

"Well, set a deadline then," urged Biddy. "If we don't hear from Cleve by Monday's mail—how's that?"

Three-year-old Molly came running into the room,

mostly mud. "Mike pushed me in the sp'inkler," she sobbed. "I fell down and I'm all over mud!"

"I'll say you are," said Biddy. "Don't touch anything."

"Never mind, baby," soothed Kate. "Get into a sunsuit and I'll take that dress down to Nora. It's time to hang out clothes anyway."

"I have to write my letter to Dave," said Biddy in a lilting voice. "I'm going to write him every single day, rain or shine."

"You're supposed to wait until he answers," said Kate.

"He'll probably never answer." Biddy's eyes filled with tears. "Torrey's father will prob'bly never let him even *see* my letters!"

"Oh for gosh sakes!" snorted Kate.

On Monday morning Torrey went down to the library after phoning for an appointment with the librarian. A pleasant-faced Negro girl from the main desk took her back to Mr. Brock's office.

"Thanks, Miss Clavel. Good morning, Miss Thorne." He rose and shook hands with her.

He's nice, thought Torrey. Nice hands, nice eyes. I like him. I wonder if he likes me. She took the chair he offered, and he sat down in the swivel chair before a desk littered with papers, books, a chart, and letters which he had been signing.

"I understand you have a college degree and a year of library school, but not a library degree, is that it?"

Torrey nodded. She did not try to explain.

"In that case we can only offer you half-time em

ployment for the present. It has been suggested that you might like to complete the credits for your degree at the same time?"

"I'd like to try."

"No reason why you can't. Want to try the half-time job for a week or two and see how it goes?"

"I haven't had much practical experience, Mr. Brock. Will there be someone to show me the ropes?"

"Clarissa Clavel, the girl who brought you in. She's a top-notch librarian. She'll help you if you need it. All library work is a mass of detail, as you must realize, after a year in library school. The thing is," he grinned as he lifted his shoulders, "not to get bogged down in routines. While books and records are important, people are more so. And children," he added, "are more important than anybody."

Torrey smiled back at him.

"The salary will be one hundred and fifty dollars for twenty hours a week. When can you start? Today?"

Torrey felt rushed off her feet. "I guess so," she faltered.

"Good! Which do you prefer, morning or afternoon?"

Torrey hadn't thought that far ahead.

"How about afternoons to start with?" Mr. Brock prompted. "Then you can see what is offered at Library School this fall. If your classes come in the morning, we can continue the arrangement, or we can shift if necessary. There are always more children here in the afternoon."

"That settles it then," agreed Torrey.

He beamed at her. "I hear you are a fine story-teller, Miss Thorne."

Torrey was surprised. Nora must have told him.

"Would you care to undertake a story hour this summer?"

"I can try."

"We've needed one for a long time. The children have been asking for it. Thursdays?"

Again Torrey felt rushed, but she didn't want to refuse. She nodded.

"Fine. I'll get it in the paper."

"Shall I come this afternoon then?"

"Might as well stay this morning, now that you're here." He pressed a buzzer. "Miss Clavel, Miss Thorne will be in the children's room half-time. Introduce her to the staff, will you, and the charging machine and anything else she needs to know? If there is any question Clarissa Clavel can't answer—which I doubt—come to me, Miss Thorne. That's what I'm here for."

The morning flew by with too many things to learn all at once. Torrey's head was spinning with the complex details of trying to run just one room in the library.

She enjoyed working with Clarissa, admiring her quick mind, her thorough knowledge, her easy and good-natured approach to the children who came in. Torrey liked the children. She enjoyed it when they let her help them find the books they wanted. Some of them just wanted to be left alone.

The noon whistle blew before she had any idea

it was that time. "Think I'll ever get it straight?" she asked Clarissa in the dressing room.

"Sure. You're doing all right. It takes some people weeks to get the hang of all those cards and numbers. And you're fine with the children."

"I made a lot of dumb mistakes."

"Everybody does when they first come in. Nobody on the outside has any idea how much there is to learn about a library."

Torrey went home feeling encouraged. She had a job she was sure she would like. She was earning money, and the thought of it lifted a nagging worry from her mind.

She walked up the long, winding street to Nora's, under the leafy trees. At the end of the second block, along the opposite side of the street, the redstone ivy-covered fence of the Clevinger estate began. Torrey knew it ran for miles up the hill. She was thinking about Miss Cluney Mary when she saw Kate, dressed in shorts and a T-shirt, waving frantically to her from Nora's gate. Kate was holding a cablegram.

Torrey ran panting up the hill. She snatched the cablegram from Kate's hand while Kate danced up and down with impatience.

"It's Cleve. He says 'Where are you why don't you write my letters are at Gang's I love you.' Oh! Kate!"

"I knew it," said Kate. "What'll you do now?"

A long, glistening black car slid gently to a stop at the curb. A chauffeur in a maroon cap and uniform with polished black boots stepped out. He opened the door. Out of the limousine stepped Biddy O'Shea.

"Thank you, Honniger," she said with a regal gesture. "That will be all."

The chauffeur lifted his cap, closed the door, opened his own, and slid with one twisting motion into the front seat. The car purred away from the curb and up the hill.

"Biddy!" said Kate. "You've been gone all morning. Where have you been?"

"I'm going to have a car and a chauffeur just like that when I'm a famous author," she crooned. "It's elegance personified."

"Where have you been?" demanded Kate again.

"Here are your letters, Torrey," said Biddy. "I told Miss Cluney Mary you wanted me to pick them up because you are busy right now being gainfully employed."

"You mean you've been up there?" demanded Kate.

"Where else? I took the telegram over the phone, so I knew where the letters were. I knew Torrey would want them as soon as possible."

Kate raised her eyes to heaven. "Come on in, Tor, and have a bite. I'll get into my other clothes. You'll have time to read your letters."

"She's going to read them to us," said Biddy.

"Oh, no, she isn't," said Kate.

"You mean I went all the way up there and bearded that ogre in her den and I don't get to hear the letters I nearly had to stab her to get?"

Torrey's laugh bubbled over. "I'll read parts of them to you, Biddy, how's that? And I want to hear everything—every single thing—that happened up there."

"She's an ogress," said Biddy. "She never would have given me those letters if I hadn't threatened her."

"Threatened her!" moaned Kate.

"Well, I was going to. But she finally came through with the letters. She could see that I meant business. I looked her right square in the eye."

Torrey read them parts of the letters during lunch. "I'll read them word for word later," she told them.

The first letter gave her Cleve's address and said he was sending the letters to Gang's. "You'll have left college by now, Torrey, and I'm not sure of your home address. I've asked Gang to forward them. Besides, I want you and Gang to know each other, and this is one way to bring you two together. She's quite a gal, Torrey, and I want you to love her as I do."

Torrey made a face and read on.

Cleve was enthusiastic about the beautiful South American city, the new job, the d'Alvarez family.

"He doesn't mention any beautiful señoritas," commented Biddy. "I'm glad of that. We have enough to worry about with Cluney Mary."

Cleve's next letter did not sound so happy. "There's too much palaver over every little thing. What I do mostly is sit around and wait. They can pass the time of day for three hours. I drink coffee until I can feel the brown beans sprouting out of my ears. I wish I'd waited until we could be mar-

111

ried, Torrey. Then I'd have you to look forward to at the end of the day."

Biddy sighed. "Isn't it romantic!"

Still another letter talked of Torrey's coming down. "I'll meet you at the boat or the airport. I won't even be coherent. I'll just babble like a fool. We can be married any way you like, civil or church. All kinds of churches down here. I don't give a rip as long as it's legal, and we can be together when it's over. They never mention money, so I don't know what I'm earning. I'm still drawing on my account up there."

The last letter was a blast at Torrey. What did she mean by not writing? Where was she? He was starved for news of her. The job was boring, the living expenses were exorbitant, the weather was cold and wet, and he hated every word of the Spanish language.

"Poor darling," said Torrey. "I'll send him a cablegram. Now, Biddy, give."

"Well," began Biddy, her eyes sparkling, "I sure settled her hash."

"Settle it quick," said Kate, "I have to leave in ten minutes."

"Well, you remember, we set a deadline."

"We did no such thing!" cried Kate.

"Well, I did. When a letter didn't come, but the telegram did, and I saw that big black car of hers go rolling down the street, I went down to the market. By the time I got there the car was parked in the lot in back of the market. It was empty, so I got in and sat in the back seat."

"Biddy, you're incorrigible!"

Biddy giggled. "I was scared she'd come out. And I wasn't sure just what I'd say if she did. But I never saw her down there. I took a chance, and it paid off. The chauffeur was surprised. He had so many packages he didn't see me until he put them in. Then he said, 'I beg your pardon, Miss!' I looked at him very haughtily. It's what he's used to. I looked him right in the eye, and I said, 'Miss Cluney Mary would like to have me pick up some mail she has at the house for Miss Thorne. Would you mind driving me up there? My car is in the garage.'"

"Why! *Biddy!*"

"That old car of Bob's is. I guess it's as much mine as anybody's. So we drove up there along miles of roads and trees and swimming pools and lawns. I was a little nervous when I got there."

"I should think you might be," said Kate. "I've never heard of such nerve."

"I'm just thankful *I* didn't have to do it," said Torrey.

"A cross-looking woman took me into the most gosh-awful room. All statues and books. And here's this woman sitting at a carved desk. She's seven feet tall, Torrey, and she has eyes that pierce right through you, and big crunching teeth."

Torrey laughed. "Don't believe her, Kate. She's not that bad."

"Don't interrupt," said Biddy. "I said, very top-lofty, 'I've come for Miss Thorne's mail, Miss Clev-inger.' I made my voice like that Dame Somebody's in the movies."

"What did she say?" asked Torrey.

"I'm coming to that. She said, and I quote, 'Let

113

me see, now, where did I put those letters?' and I said, 'Miss Thorne has a cablegram that says you have them, so don't stall.' "

"Oh Biddy! You didn't!" Kate was appalled.

"I did too. She asked me where was Miss Thorne, and I said she was too busy to come because she was getting a new job at the library. That surprised her. She got up and went out, and when she came back she had the letters."

"What did she say?" asked Torrey again.

"Well, she said, 'Tell Miss Thorne I am sorry I was unable to get the letters to her sooner.' And I said 'We'll let bygones be bygones,' and she said would I like some light refreshment, and I said, 'No, thank you, it's a long way home,' and she said, 'Honniger will take you,' and he did. I'd be walking until Christmas if he hadn't."

"See what I mean?" said Kate. "Murder!"

"I'm glad to get the letters, Biddy," Torrey told her. "It's a big load off my mind. I think you've been wonderful."

"Good enough for Dave?"

"In another five or six years."

"He'll have one foot in the grave by then."

"But think how much more sense you'll have."

"She'll never have a lick of sense," mourned Kate. "I have to run. Have supper with us tonight, Tor. Nora'll want to hear all about it. She's not going to be pleased about Biddy."

"I can't eat with you all the time."

"Get some lamb patties if it will make you feel better."

"Get wieners," begged Biddy. "We *never* have them."

Torrey bought the wieners Biddy wanted. When she found out how much they cost for nine people, she realized what her father had meant when he said that food didn't grow on trees.

She eyed the remaining greenbacks with concern. She had been in Marysdale only three days, and she was already short of funds. She had a few staples stacked up on the shelves of her tiny kitchen, and some canned goods. She'd never last the month out at this rate.

There was a telephone call for her when she got back. She called the number, thinking it might be someone at the library. Instead, over the hubbub in the living room, she heard Miss Cluney Mary's voice. Torrey managed to kick the door shut against the barking dogs.

"Miss Thorne? This is Miss Clevinger. I called about your letters. I wanted to make sure you have them."

"Yes, thank you." Torrey's voice was cool and detached.

"The young person who came here—it was very kind of her—gave me the impression that you expect to be employed at the libr'y here?"

"Yes. I'll be on half-time in the children's room."

"That is what you wanted to do, wasn't it? Get that sort of a situation? I'm glad of that."

Torrey made a face into the telephone. A half-time job because of you, she was thinking.

"Now about your mail, Miss Thorne. I am sorry there was a delay. You see I have been gone for

115

ten days on a visit in Carmel. I didn't intend to stay so long, so my mail was not forwarded. On my return last evening I was concerned about how to put in motion some means of locating you, when this extraordinary child turned up. I'm very grateful to her. She was quite stern with me, really."

"I hope she wasn't rude."

"No. Just firm. She seemed to think I had been holding the mail, and I wanted you to know that there was no way of knowing, while in Carmel, that there were letters here for you."

"That's quite all right, Miss Clevinger. I was just glad to get them."

"Was there—was there any special news?"

Torrey was surprised at the yearning in the voice. She was about to say no, nothing special. Then she changed her mind. "Would you like to hear the letters?" she asked with warmth in her own voice.

"I'd love to share some of your news bits, if you would."

Torrey read the parts of the letters she wanted to share with Miss Cluney Mary.

"Thank you, my dear. Clevinger is having quite an exciting experience, isn't he?"

Torrey didn't answer.

"I hope we meet again soon, Miss Thorne, now that you are close at hand?"

There was a question at the end of this remark, but Torrey ignored it. There was an awkward little pause.

"Well, good-by, m'dear."

"Good-by, Miss Clevinger." Torrey cradled the

phone. I wasn't very nice, she was thinking; I wish I'd been nicer.

The next morning a box arrived for Torrey from Mom. It was full of all sorts of pleasant surprises. Dried figs, cookies, nut bread, canned fruit, home canned turkey and chicken, cucumber pickles, and pickled olives. It looked like enough to eat for weeks. Torrey's eyes sparkled. Trust Mom to know an empty bin when she saw one.

There was a loving but cautious scribble. Torrey gathered that Dad was still furious with her. Also Mom wanted to know about linens and bedding. "I'll send you the things you used at college, Torrey; they're still in the boxes."

This would be a real lift. On top of this there was a letter from Dave, with another twenty dollars in it, and stern notice that she was to keep him posted about money. Maybe with all this she could make a go of it until she got her first salary check. Then, she was sure, she could pay it all back.

The next afternoon Torrey spent learning about a library. There seemed to be no end to the things she had to learn, details of filing and sorting and shelving. She had learned the principles behind these various processes at Library School, but ease of application would come only with practice. Also, each library had certain rules and arrangements of its own. These had been found to work at some time and had been carried along through the years because it would involve too much time and trouble to change them.

Torrey caught herself saying more than once, "We didn't do it that way in Library School."

Clarissa would grin at her. "I know, but it is the way we do it here."

Library work meant, she found, a lot of bending and stooping. She was aching all over by the time a page came to say tea was ready. It was fun to sit in the crowded little room that reeked of coffee and shellac, a room painted a vivid, shocking pink.

"Wow!" said Torrey.

"Giddy, isn't it?" said one of the others.

"Better than that *café au lait* mixed with grime that we used to have," drawled another.

"I'll be around to collect a quarter for the gift fund," said a tall woman whose face was a mass of wrinkles from her hair line to her chin.

"And we have to put a quarter in every week for the coffee fund," said a bright-looking girl with a bouncing, black pony tail.

"By the time you pay ALA dues and CLA dues and ACL dues and hospitalization and taxes and all these extras, you can put your take-home pay in your pipe and not even blow smoke rings," grumbled a woman with one shoulder higher than the other and eyebrows that met in a deep frown. "It'll be tough on you, Thorne, on half-time. I'd never make ends meet if my husband didn't have a job."

Torrey refused to let it worry her. She dropped the two quarters in the tin cans with slots cut in them. She enjoyed the cookies that Clarissa had brought, and the coffee someone else had made.

She was tired at five o'clock, but not as tired as she had been the day before. She met Clarissa at the lockers. "You weren't around much today, Clarissa."

"I was busy, and I could see you were doing all right by yourself. Did you see the notice in the paper about the story hour?"

"No!"

"You can see it at the desk in the morning. Mona clips everything, but she's gone by now."

"What did it say?"

"Says you're a storyteller and you'll be here every Thursday afternoon at four P.M. in the Story Hour Room."

"I'm scared silly."

"You don't need to be. Tell a couple of stories you know real well. It's a good sign if you're nervous. You'll do better because of it. Most artists react like that."

"You flatter me," said Torrey. But she felt warmed by the other girl's interest.

"You have a storyteller's voice," said Clarissa. "I could listen to it all day. We're in luck. We've needed a storyteller for so long, and now at last we have one."

12

TORREY LIKED HER JOB. She liked most of the staff.
They were friendly and helpful, laughing at her
mistakes, answering her questions with patience.

When she took some of Mom's dried figs down
for tea, they fell upon them with yelps of joy. Torrey already felt a part of a pleasant organization
where most of the staff were interesting and intelli-
gent people, working hard at highly technical jobs.

There were two or three who puzzled her. There
was Mona, the reference librarian. She was a tall,
slender girl with a face as finely etched as a feather.
Her silver-gold hair was brushed back in two shining wings that met in a neat duck's tail at the back.
Her words were clipped and sometimes sharp. Her
clothes were in soft, muted shades, expensively
tailored, and she never wore the same thing two
days running.

Mona could be witty at the expense of others,
both public and staff. "The cockeyed questions I

get asked! A woman asked me if we had the book, *Three Men on a Horse*, by David Belasco. What she wanted was *The Four Horsemen of the Apocalypse*, by Blasco-Ibáñez. And here's a written request for *Who's Your Schoolmaster?* You have to be a mind reader."

But Torrey could see that Mona was as tireless as a hired detective in running down information, in finding for the many writers who haunted the library that extra book on Africa, or whether Passover, in 1906, preceded or followed the earthquake.

There was worried-looking Hertha Boatwright, in the branch department. Mrs. Boatwright always took her cookies or cake back to her own desk. "I'll eat them a little later," she would murmur.

"Take two," Mona would urge.

With an apologetic little laugh Hertha would take another piece of candy or an extra slice of cake and go off by herself.

Torrey thought her greedy and selfish, and she thought Mona was being sarcastic.

There was Warren Brock, the chief librarian. Torrey wondered about him. He seldom came to the staff room. When he did, he would bolt a cup of coffee and go off again. He seemed pleasant enough, and Torrey could often hear him laughing in his office with visitors. She learned from Clarissa that he had a little girl of six, and that his wife had died several years before.

Clarissa told Torrey to take time out to find stories to tell. "That's the most important part of storytelling," she said. "You win half the battle right there. Do you keep track of your stories and where you found them? It will save you hours of time later."

Torrey remembered Dr. Jordan's emphasis on selection, and his insistence that his students keep records. She had pleased him when she showed him the five-year diary she intended to use, keeping track of the seasons and holidays that way, but he had expected her to keep a card file as well.

She decided to tell "The Gunniwolf" and one of Howard Pyle's fairy tales. She had told several of them in class and had listened in delight to others. She liked his picture-making words and his humor. She couldn't find "Clever Peter and the Two Bottles," but from his *Wonder Clock* she chose the story of "Peterkin and the Little Gray Hare." The pattern of the story was easy to visualize, and, having learned it once, it came back to her as she read it and told it out loud.

As the time drew near for the story hour, Torrey felt her nerves tighten. Her throat was dry. Her hands were clammy. She tried to think of the beginning of her second story and had a blank moment of panic when she couldn't remember how it went. She wished she hadn't agreed to tell stories.

She went into the story room and looked at the empty chairs. They looked stiff and solemn, in straight-backed rows. She began pulling them around in a semicircle.

Clarissa came in with an armload of picture books. "That's much better. Going to sit or stand?"

Torrey pondered this. "If there's just a few, I'll sit. If not I'd rather stand, so I can see all their faces."

Clarissa nodded. "I've brought you some of the

new books that have just gone through. It breaks the ice, and the children love to see them."

A small girl poked her head in at the door. "Is they stories?" she asked.

"There will be," said Torrey.

"Yes, they is," whispered the small girl, and two more youngsters sidled around the door.

"Come in," urged Torrey.

Solemnly they sat down in the second row. Torrey beamed at them, but they only stared back at her, until her smile faltered. I haven't proved myself yet, she thought.

More children filtered in until there were about a dozen. Torrey thought she should wait a little longer, but Clarissa came briskly in. "This is Torrey Thorne, children. She's our new storyteller. She always starts her story hour smack on time, so you come early again next Thursday. You can wait in the Children's Room and look at books."

Mr. Brock came in and took a seat at the back of the room. His friendly smile steadied Torrey as she held the new books up for the children to see.

Their comments tickled her, and she forgot to be self-conscious. She slid easily into "The Gunniwolf" and was surprised and delighted to hear them laugh outright. She outdid herself with Peterkin, to their great delight.

The children took out all the books that Clarissa had brought. Torrey had the satisfaction of stamping them out at the desk in the Children's Room.

"They had a good time at the story hour, Torrey," said Clarissa. "We could hear them clear out here. Maybe you'll have a bigger crowd next week. These'll pass the word."

Torrey was remembering what Dr. Jordan had said. "Storytellers always prefer a small audience. It is easier to become *en rapport* with a small group."

"We're so pleased." Clarissa's voice was warm with approval. "I'm looking ahead to the stories myself."

Torrey tried out her next week's stories on the three little children at Nora's. She and Nora put them to bed, and Torrey told them the stories after they were safely tucked in. Biddy came too, draping herself beside her mother across the fourth bed, while Torrey sat at small Molly's feet.

She knew that the stories she was telling were too old for these children, if she counted their years. But they were long conditioned to stories, fierce ones, and they listened with relish to the tale of "The Princess on the Glass Hill," with its refrain, "If it isn't worse than this, I daresay I can stand it out."

The next morning Biddy came out to Torrey's room. She had a sheaf of papers in her hand, an embarrassed look in her eye. "Torrey, read this and see if it's any good?" She pushed the papers into Torrey's hand and fled.

Torrey put down her broom and looked through the papers. They were badly typed, with no margins, single-spaced, and the spelling had been done by ear. But Torrey's eyes opened wide as she read down the page.

It was an Irish story of a small white kid—a story

as Irish as a leprechaun, absurdly simple and highly entertaining, by Bridget O'Shea.

Torrey carried it back to the big house. She found Biddy in the living room looking sulky and bored, her legs draped over the end of the davenport.

"This is a good story, Biddy."

"No kidding?"

"I think it's delightful. I'd like to learn it and try it with a small group in the library someday, just to see if it tells as well as it reads. The littlest ones would love it."

Biddy bounced off the davenport. "Is it that good?"

"I like it. I think it needs cutting. For this age it should be nearly all action. Mind if I learn it to tell?"

"Gosh, no. You can have it. Wish I had a more interesting name for an author. Bridget O'Shea. Isn't it awful!"

"I don't think so. If I were you, I'd use plain Biddy. Biddy O'Shea. It's not like anybody else's."

"It's so darn Irish!"

Torrey laughed. "You can't help that. Think of all the wonderful Irish stories you can write with a name like that."

"Granny tells some corkers."

"Get them down, Biddy. Get them down—before it's too late." Torrey hesitated, and then she said, "Haven't you any friends around here, Biddy?"

Biddy made a face and flopped back on the davenport. "Nope. They've all gone to scout camp. All but me. No money."

"Boys too?"

"Lumber camps, some of them, or summer resorts or working."

"Next year why don't you earn your camp money? Lots of girls do."

"What can you get to do around here?"

"I don't know, but I'd sure find out. I waited on tables two years at Yosemite and had a whale of a good time."

"It's an idea," said Biddy, picking up her magazine.

Torrey's second story hour was easier. There were twenty children and again they seemed to like her stories. She showed Lynd Ward's "The Biggest Bear" this time and told the story as she turned the pages.

Again Mr. Brock had come to listen in. Afterward he stayed to talk with her. "I can see that the children enjoy your stories. Miss Clavel tells me you have a gift for handling children."

"They're lots of fun."

"Fine. Dr. Jordan was right when he told me you were a topnotch storyteller."

"Dr. Jordan!"

"Yes. He was the one who suggested you for part-time work when he heard we needed someone. He said you would want to pick up those credits you need in your free time."

Torrey took the long hill home in a daze. She couldn't get over it. Dr. Jordan had failed her in his course. He had prevented her getting her degree. Now he had recommended her as a topnotch storyteller.

Life, Torrey was thinking, was certainly full of unexpected somersaults.

13

TORREY FELT THAT THE CHILDREN'S ROOM of the Marysdale Library was her very own. It was an old-fashioned room, with odd angles and high windows, with a grimy patina accumulated through years of neglect on the part of an indifferent city council and public. Where pictures had hung at one time the wall was lighter in color. Above the furnace there was a fan of dark discoloration. A small room had been built in one corner to house the California adult collection. This was known as the "Dungeon."

But in spite of the drab walls and the lack of space, there was warmth to the room. Fresh flowers from Nora's garden helped, and Torrey kept patterns of bright jackets in the spaces above the bookcases. She encouraged the children to bring things to display—model airplanes, rocks, and arrowheads. She found books about these things and kept them moving.

The books themselves are beautiful, thought Torrey—and the children.

This was her stamping ground, her own field of endeavor from which she could work with the children, listen to them, learn their names and hobbies, and find out what they wanted to read. She often wondered about the children who didn't come to the library. So many didn't. How could they be reached, these Johnnies who probably could read, but who didn't? Did they get books enough in their school libraries? Did they have books at home? Torrey couldn't imagine a childhood without books or libraries.

A little boy came in with his application filled out. Torrey told him his library card would be waiting for him the next time he came.

"Can't I take a book then?" he asked.

"Yes. Go find one you like"—she glanced at the blank in her hand—"Jimmy."

He went off to the picture-book section and sat on the floor, absorbed in Thidwick, the big moose with all sorts of weird creatures on his horns.

"How could he do that?" he asked Torrey when she came by with her truck.

"Must be magic, huh? Let's take the book to a table, Jimmy; the light's better there. On the floor you might tear the pages, turning them against your clothes."

He rose obediently, but he didn't see her. He walked to the nearest table, never taking his eyes from the book, like a sleepwalker.

Torrey remembered herself when Mom would ask her to set the table and she was still inside the walls of a little house on the prairie with Laura and Mary and Pa.

Books and children and stories. This was Torrey's life now. There were many compensations in it. Working with children could be very satisfying.

As she chose her stories she could see Dr. Jordan stroking his beard as he said, "Never tell a story you don't enjoy yourself. Dislike of the story will edge through to your audience." So she chose stories that held a real appeal for her. "Tell fierce ones," Granny had said. Torrey decided that fierce ones and funny ones were the ones she liked. She hunted for them through the collections in the library, finding them among the ancient tales in the new collections of stories from many lands.

Sometimes the long afternoons were tiring. Torrey wasn't used to so much bending and stooping. Books were heavy. There were times when she felt depressed. She wondered how she could stick it out, working day after day, spending so much of her free time learning stories to tell, when she might be happily married to Cleve.

By four o'clock, after the first wave of children had come and gone, Torrey felt free to take her fifteen-minute breather. Mona and Clarissa nearly always joined her. At that hour they usually had the staff room to themselves.

On Monday, when Torrey had seen Jimmy off with Thidwick, she let the girl at the main desk know that she would be away for a few minutes. She heaved a sigh of weariness as she went down to the staff room with Clarissa on her heels. She found Mona cutting into a towering three-layer lemon cake.

"Whoops! Where did that gorgeous pile of calories come from?"

"Mrs. Field," answered Clarissa, heading for the washroom for some paper towels to use for plates. "She's a friend of Mona's. She's always sending things in. She likes us."

Mona deftly flipped a wedge of cake onto a paper towel. "I help her with research. She's writing a book on Indiana. Half the people on this Peninsula are writing books on something. It's a disease."

Hertha Boatwright came in from the catalogue room. Her eyes lit up at sight of the cake. "Boy! Am I glad I waited!" She pushed a strand of hair from behind her glasses. "Any tea?"

"Probably cold," answered Clarissa, "but there's hot water. Make some fresh with a tea bag."

Clarissa produced a sheet of waxed paper and Mona cut a generous slice of cake and wrapped it up.

Hertha came back with her steaming cup of tea. "Come to think of it," she said with an apologetic little laugh, "I'm not very hungry. I won't eat the cake just now. Would it be all right if I cut a small piece to take back to my desk?"

"I've wrapped a piece up for you," said Mona. "Sit down and have some with us. No argument."

Hertha ate every crumb of the cake Mona cut for her. When she was gone with her wrapped piece held carefully in her hands, Torrey asked, "Can we all have extras?"

"Nope." Mona's voice was lowered. "That's for Hertha's little girl. She's at the C.P. School."

"What's that?"

"The School for Cerebral Palsied Children. Hertha takes some of the stuff we get here home to Cindy. She hasn't any time to do any baking, and she can't afford to buy stuff all the time."

Torrey was ashamed of her original estimate of Hertha Boatwright.

That night Torrey went over Biddy's story about the naughty little white goat. With the eye of a storyteller she blue-penciled it right and left. Then she went over to Nora's.

"Where's Biddy?" she asked.

Nora was untying bibs and lifting Molly and Mike down from their high chairs. She looked flushed and tired. "I don't know," she said in a worried voice. "She didn't come home to dinner." She raised her voice. "Did Biddy tell you where she was going, Granny?"

The old woman twisted away from the table, rocking a little to get on her feet and then sinking back again. "No, I don't know about Biddy. She had me tellin' stories all mornin'. Cuchulain and the fiery wheel I told her, and a story of Finn McCool. After lunch I was mebbe asleep. Is she missin'?"

"Yes. It's not like Biddy. She's lazy and gatless half the time, but she wouldn't do anything to worry us. I have to go off to a meeting, and I don't want to go without her or Kate here, either one."

"I'll stay," offered Torrey.

Nora frowned. "I can't afford a baby sitter, Torrey. It's murder."

"I'll earn some of the meals I've had in this house,"

said Torrey. "And maybe Granny'll tell me about the Irish stories."

Granny nodded. "There's good stories out of Ireland. The Irish tell fierce stories, Torrey Thorne, woven of great deeds and little ones, with love and sorrow and laughter and death in the weft of them, and words of color and strength for the woof. There's the bigness of the saints and the heroes, and the spite and mischief of the 'little people.' The strong thread of everlasting truth follows through the pattern. Treat an Irish story with care, Torrey Thorne, it has the breath of life in it."

The old woman rocked to her feet, and Torrey slid a firm hand under the frail elbow.

Nora had gone off to change, and Torrey saw the old woman to the hall doorway.

Granny stood there, her hand on her stick, her faded blue eyes peering up into Torrey's face. "The Irish seanachies put their feet to the road and carried the tales with them from here to there. You'll find the roots of them in stories the world over. I lay it on ye, Torrey Thorne, to carry them with ye wherever you go. Many a long road's been shortened by a good story." She turned and stumped off down the hall, the blackthorn stick punching into the hall carpet.

Torrey put the babies to bed and told them "The Three Bears" and "The Gunniwolf." Afterward she sat in the comfortable, shabby living room and watched the coals of Granny's fire turn gray. Where was Biddy? Torrey was worried because it was quite dark now. She wished she knew someone to call. Dennis came in from playing ball.

"Know where we can call about Biddy?" asked Torrey.

"No."

Kate came in, tired from a long day of practice teaching. "Drat that young one," she said when Torrey told her Biddy was missing. "Dennis, have you seen Biddy?"

"No."

"Have a good time at the game?"

"No."

"Why not?"

"Too slow. And afterward all the kids I knew went off to get hot dogs with their dads."

Kate sighed as the front door opened and Biddy limped in. "Where've you been?" demanded Kate. "You've had us all in a dither."

Biddy plumped down on Granny's hassock.

"Want some supper?" asked Kate.

"I've had supper."

"Where?"

"I don't have to tell you, but I have a job." Biddy eased her feet out of her flats, massaging her toes tenderly. "For filthy lucre. I ate there."

"What kind of a job," demanded Kate.

"I'm a carhop. I'm waiting on cars at the drive-in. Torrey told me to."

"Biddy O'Shea, I did not."

"You said I should have earned some money for camp. It's too late for camp. But money's money. We could use some."

"You should have asked Nora," said Kate.

"No, I shouldn't. There's only one way to get a

133

job. Not talk about it, just go get it. You know what one man said?"

"I can imagine!" Kate's voice was withering.

"No, you can't. He didn't say how pretty I am. I just laugh when they do. It disarms them. If they get any further, I give 'em the frozen glare—after they've paid. No, this man said, 'This is the best meal I've tasted all across the country, and it isn't the food, it's the service.' So there. And he gave me a dollar tip. Cool!"

"Do you like it?" asked Torrey.

"I don't know yet. It's hard work. The trays are heavy, and your feet hurt, and there aren't enough girls to go around, and the people in cars get cross, and Mr. Towser—"

"Mr. *Who*?" demanded Kate.

"Towser, that's his name. It's the holy truth. He runs the joint. He's always saying, 'Get a move on, girls, you're slow as molasses,' and all the time we're running our legs off, and I think the uniforms aren't a bit smart. But you get paid every week, and I get a lot of tips because I'm pretty and act shy." Biddy chuckled. "So, Torrey, 'if it doesn't get any worse than this, I can stand it.'"

"What's Biddy talking about?" asked Kate.

Torrey laughed. "That's what Cinderlad said in 'The Princess on the Glass Hill' when the barn began to rock."

When Torrey went off to her room she was thinking if Biddy can stand a job as a carhop at a drive-in, I certainly ought to be able to stand a half-time job at the library.

134

Where love is great, the littlest doubts are fears

WILLIAM SHAKESPEARE—HAMLET

14

THE NEXT MORNING brought a long letter from Cleve. He had heard from Torrey, and his letter was full of plans. He didn't say much about Chile or his work, and Torrey debated with herself about calling Miss Cluney Mary. Then, remembering the yearning in that voice over the phone, she went over to Nora's and dialed the number.

"The Clevinger residence," said a flat voice. "Who is speaking?"

"This is Torrey Thorne, Mrs. Jones. Is Miss Clevinger there?"

"I couldn't say, Miss Thorne. I'll inquire."

Torrey waited a long time. "She better come pretty soon," she muttered. "I'm getting cold feet."

"Yes, Miss Thorne?"

"Good morning, Miss Clevinger."

"Yes, Miss Thorne?"

"I had a letter from Cleve this morning, Miss Clevinger. I thought—that is—you might like—at least—" Oh, for heaven's sake, you dimwit, get on with it!

"Thank you, Miss Thorne. It was very kind of you to call. But I also have a letter from Clevinger."

"Good! Then you—"

"He seems to be entering into the life there, doesn't he? He tells me he hopes to go skiing, and he has joined a folk-dancing group of young people."

"Oh?"

"I didn't realize that Clevinger was interested in folk dancing. Such an old-fashioned art. It was great fun in my day, the 'Lancers' and 'the Barn Dance' and 'the Virginia Reel.' We could use some wholesome fun like that in this country, it seems to me."

"But we—"

"I do appreciate your calling, Miss Thorne. Goodbye and thank you."

When Torrey had hung up she read Cleve's letter again. It was full of love for her, plans for their future, questions about her job. But there was not one word about skiing or folk dancing with young people.

Torrey had debated whether or not to tell Cleve about the ring, about her own family's reaction to her engagement, about losing her degree. She had decided against it, at least in the first letters that reached him.

Now she sat down at her typewriter and got it all down. She tempered her views of Miss Cluney Mary, but the facts were there. She didn't minimize her father's anger, but she glowed over the hope chest and Dave's help.

"That's the situation, Cleve," she wrote in conclusion. "Miss Cluney Mary has your ring. She and I are not on unfriendly terms. We are on no terms whatever. My father is furious, and I won't go home until he stops raving about you. The one bright spot in my life is this family here. I love every one of them, especially Kate and the unpredictable Biddy O'Shea.

"I love you, Cleve, more than words can tell. But I don't think I can come down there and marry you. We have to straighten out this tangle with Miss Cluney Mary and with my father first."

The next morning Torrey took Biddy's story over to Nora's again. But Biddy was sleeping the sleep of the just—and the employed.

Kate was cleaning up the kitchen, grumbling, "We won't get another lick of work out of those two young ones. Dennis is inspired too. He's gone off to get some lawns to mow. They're going to make a million dollars and buy Nora a dishwasher."

On an impulse, Torrey typed up Biddy's story in proper manuscript form. Then she tucked it in an envelope and mailed it off to a juvenile magazine. If it's good enough to tell, she told herself, it's good enough to sell.

When Torrey got down to the library there was a note on her desk: "Please see Mr. Brock when you come in."

Now what? thought Torrey as she circled around the main desk and through the stacks to Mr. Brock's office.

"Come in, Miss Thorne."

Torrey was thinking, he's like Cleve, a little. Those wings of white hair give him a distinguished look.

You can tell he's a scholar. She sat down on the edge of a chair by his desk.

He picked up a round glass paperweight and turned it so that the snow flew about the little figures inside. "We've hit a small snag," he was saying, "in your appointment. I don't know if you understand the situation we have here. We have a library board. Up until now they've given me free rein in hiring new personnel." He put down the paperweight. "For some reason they seem to think I should have consulted them on so important a position as children's librarian."

Torrey's heart sank. Was she to lose this job, her funny children's room that seemed so surely hers, her story hour? She waited.

"The story hour is working out, isn't it?" Mr. Brock put his fingertips together and tilted back in his office chair.

"The children are fun, and they seem interested, but"—Torrey was trying to be honest—"we don't have very many of them."

He nodded. "It's our location. The city has grown up around us. We're hemmed in by arterials and the freeway. Parents hesitate to send their children down here on foot, and parking gets worse by the minute. That's why we have branches in the residential areas."

Again Torrey waited. This didn't sound as though she might lose her job.

"It seems to me we could use more than one story hour," Mr. Brock went on. "How would you like to go up to the branch at Las Pulgas and start

138

a story hour up there? You'll find Stella Stanley enthusiastic and helpful."

"I'd love it. But what about the library board?"

"Oh, that. Don't worry." He grinned boyishly. "If she starts bucking me on this, we'll have to have a showdown."

"She?"

"Miss Cluney Mary Clevinger. She's chairman of the board this year. Miss Clevinger occasionally likes to throw her weight around. We're used to it. Took me a little by surprise this time. Call Mrs. Stanley and pick your day."

Torrey hesitated. "That branch is a long way from here, isn't it? I don't have a car."

"You can take the station wagon." He smiled at her, and they both stood up. "We have a meeting of the library board this evening," he said casually. "Your appointment will be approved, I'm sure."

Torrey wasn't at all sure. If she's going to cost me a job as well as a degree, she was thinking— and then she pulled up short. Nobody but Torrey Thorne cost you that degree, she told herself.

She went back to the children's room, not knowing whether to be excited over the prospect of a new and larger story hour or scared stiff about the library board. There's nothing you can do about it, she told herself. If she wants to put you out, that's it. Live for today and let tonight take care of itself.

She began to plan the new story hour. She called Mrs. Stanley at Las Pulgas Branch.

"I'm simply thrilled!" Mrs. Stanley's voice was warm and friendly. "Mona tells me you're tops."

"I'm just learning," Torrey said, "but I love it."

"How about Tuesdays?"

"Fine. Shall I notify the paper?"

"Sure," said Stella Stanley, "but telling 'em will get 'em here faster. About three-thirty to four? They're usually here by then."

Clarissa and Mona were talking earnestly in the staff room when she came in. They stopped self-consciously.

"Where's that licking good cake?" Torrey asked.

"Listen to an optimist!" scoffed Mona. "With all these vultures? Did Brock come through with another story hour?"

"Sure did. Do I have you to thank for it?"

"Just your own abilities. I live in Las Pulgas. I'll call all the mothers I know."

"Thanks. But he also told me the board might not approve my appointment, so you'd better wait."

Mona and Clarissa glanced at each other. Mona spoke up. "I think, Torrey Thorne, you are about to provide us with a *cause célèbre*. Warren Brock's been dying to call Clevinger's bluff for lo! these many years. It's ridiculous for a library to have to kowtow to anybody. We preach freedom of speech, freedom to read what we choose, and then let a narrow-gauge person like Clevinger dictate our policies. I told him if she gets by with this, Clarissa and I'll go up there and tear her apart."

"Well, but—" began Torrey.

"Don't worry. It won't come to a showdown. People like Cluney Mary can't stand being stood up to. With another story hour booming—and boy! will it boom!—she won't have a leg left."

"I hate to make trouble—"

140

Clarissa grinned. "It isn't you who's making the trouble."

Mona pushed across a box of crackers. "Nothing fancy. Help yourself. I have to go dig up some stuff for Henry Jasmine." She went in to wash her cup and then off down the hall.

Torrey nibbled a cracker. "Awfully nice of Mona to put in a word for me. I never know quite how to take her. She's so—well, sort of—blunt."

"I know. But when Mona feels like it, she won't leave a stone unturned to help somebody. All the writers ask for her. She finds the answers in the oddest places. She has a mind like a steel trap."

"Why do you suppose she went to bat for me?"

"Probably because she likes you."

"Is she always so breezy?"

"M-m-mmm."

Torrey laughed. "Don't get lofty, Clarissa. The sixteen-year-old at the place where I'm staying says she doesn't gossip about people, she just analyzes them. I'm trying to analyze Mona. I want to know her better."

Clarissa relaxed. "Mona's okay. She's unhappy right now because her family has been needling her to come out at the Debutantes' Ball next Christmas. Mona's not interested."

"If they have that kind of money, why does she work down here?"

"Same reason you and I do. We happen to like libraries and books and people. There are lots of other jobs. Some of them pay better, some have better vacations. But I don't know any work that gives

141

you the satisfaction that this kind of work does. Mona feels the same way."

"I should think an attractive girl like that would have been snatched up long since by some man."

Clarissa drank up the last of her coffee and poured herself another half cup. "Maybe she just hasn't found the right one. It takes two. We all thought Mona was interested last year. She went out a lot with a grand guy. He's related in some way to Miss Cluney Mary Clevinger, adopted or something."

Torrey choked on her coffee. Clarissa didn't notice. "We try to sic Mona on Miss Clevinger every time she comes in. It's the only way we can keep Cluney Mary out of our hair. Mona steers her away from the new junk and into something folksy and humorous."

"Was Mona crazy about this boy last year?"

"Mona? You can't always tell about her. She makes fun of things till you can't be sure if she means it or not. She laughs at herself and everybody else. But Miss Cluney Mary Clevinger was sure pushing that romance. She was in and out of here every few days, and she had Mona up at her big house as often as Mona would go."

"Did this—this man—was he interested in Mona?"

"I don't see how he could help it, do you? He took her out a lot. Then they went to night clubs and off skiing and folk dancing. None of us knew what happened."

"I did."

"You did what?"

"Know what happened. To Clevinger Macklin.

I'm the one who's engaged to Cleve Macklin."

"Torrey!"

"Don't tell, will you, 'Rissa? I don't know why I've told you. I didn't mean to tell anyone—yet. It just popped out."

Clarissa put down her cup. "That's a tidy little tidbit you just let fall from your ruby lips, Torrey Thorne. This place would buzz like a busted beehive."

"I don't see why you shouldn't know." But Torrey couldn't help wishing she hadn't told.

"Is he here? Are you planning to get married soon?"

"No. He's in South America for a year. He wants me to go down to Santiago and marry him."

"Going?"

"I don't know." Now, more than ever, Torrey was thinking, I don't know. "I haven't made up my mind."

"Is Cluney Mary pleased about it?"

"Nope. She'll probably express her displeasure this evening at the library board. I think she'd like Cleve to marry money."

"I hope it works out for you." Clarissa's voice was warm with interest but doubtful. "And you can trust me to keep mum about it, though it's asking an awful lot."

Torrey was busy the rest of the afternoon, finding books for the children and straightening up after them. But churning through the back of her mind were the words, "night clubs and skiing and folk dancing," and then the overtones of Miss Cluney Mary's voice, "Clevinger hopes to go skiing, and he

143

has joined a folk-dancing group of young people."

As she started home, Torrey was thinking, That's the way Cleve met me, and I stole him from Mona. Now he'll meet some South American girl who can dance like fury, or some American girl down there in Chile with money, and she'll steal him just as easily away from me.

Her heart said, You don't really love Cleve if you doubt him like this, but her head said, You only knew Cleve Macklin a few weeks, Torrey Thorne. How do you know what he's really like?

Life and death upon one tether
And running beautiful together

ROBERT COFFIN—CRYSTAL MOMENT

15

THE NEXT DAY was Saturday, and Torrey had no way of knowing whether her appointment had been approved or whether she was out of a job.

I want to work with children and books, she told herself as she tied the belt of her blue housecoat and ran a comb through her dark hair. It's what I want to do. It's what I've been trained for, degree or not.

She plugged in the coffee pot and opened a can of orange juice, noting with a little feeling of panic that it was her last can. "Where did they all go?" she muttered.

She sat down at the small table, looking out across the fields of the seminary to the hills beyond. She lifted her purse from the chair in back of her and pulled out the paper money, smoothing it flat on the table.

"Where did it all go?" she asked out loud.

"Where did what go?" said a masculine voice behind her.

Torrey whirled around. "Dave!" she hastily covered the few bills on the table with a plate. "You scared the wits out of me."

"Shouldn't leave your door open."

It was wonderful to see him. He brought her all sorts of things. Linens, blankets, her reading lamp, books, extra clothes she needed, and a huge box of ranch food.

Biddy, in shabby shorts and a fluttering shirttail, helped unpack the car. Her bare feet had the toenails painted green. Her black hair was fresh-washed and shining.

"How'd you know I needed all this?" Torrey asked Dave.

"Biddy wrote me." He grinned at Biddy. "She tells me all. I know about Miss Cluney Mary and the letters. I know all about the story hours. I know about the drive-in and what it does to feet. I even know about Cuchulain and the hounds."

Biddy looked pleased with herself. "I'm practicing on Dave to be a great author. If I can make *him* see it, I can make anybody see it."

"I read the letters to Mom," said Dave. "She likes them as well as I do."

"Omigosh!" groaned Biddy.

"She says it's a pity you can't spell."

"I'll have a secretary to proofread my stuff," answered Biddy with dignity.

"Mom sent a picnic basket," he went on. "She thought we all might like to drive to the coast."

"What fun!" said Torrey.

"We couldn't all go," said Nora. "There's too many for one car."

"Can't we rent a car?" asked Dave.

"I'll borrow one for you down the street," offered Biddy. "Only I can't go."

"Can't go?" Dave's voice held real regret.

"Nope. Saturdays and Sundays are our big days. I'd lose my job."

"Well, but—" began Dave. He looked sheepishly at Torrey. His face said, plain to read, that the picnic had been planned for Biddy.

"We could have a breakfast picnic," suggested Nora. "Tomorrow morning. If we get up at five. We can be at the beach by six. If we eat early we can swim from nine to ten. It may be too cold anyway. We can hike. What time do you have to be at the drive-in, Biddy?"

"My shift is from noon to eight, with time out for food around five-thirty."

"If we leave the beach by eleven, we can make it."

Dave hefted the basket. "There's salad in here. And cake and cookies. Not breakfast foods."

"Who cares?" said Biddy. "I peeked, and there's chicken too. Fried chicken!" Her eyes rolled in ecstasy. "I'll gnaw a drumstick on the way back to the drive-in."

"Better get it all in the refrigerator," said Nora, "if we aren't going to use it until tomorrow."

"If there's no picnic," said Dave, "I'd like to drive to the city. Anybody want to go?"

Torrey did. She wanted a chance to talk to Dave. Biddy went off to change. When she came back her green toenails showed through the tips of her red sandals.

"Go take that goo off your feet," Dave ordered. "You look like a lit Christmas tree."

"Yes, sir—no, sir; oh, sir—aye, sir!" Biddy turned to Torrey. "Is he always so bossy with his women?"

Dave showed his teeth in a snarl. "I beat them with sticks!"

"O-ooo-oooh!"

"Git!" he ordered, and Biddy got.

"We'd still have time to go to Wolf Ridge, for some folk dancing tonight," suggested Kate. "After Biddy's through. Things never really get swinging up there until ten-thirty or so."

"I'll stay here," said Nora, "with the little ones."

"Oh, no, you won't! They'll be in bed and out for the count by eight. Granny won't mind, will you?"

"Wish I could go too." The old woman's voice was wistful.

"Why not?" asked Dave. "Let's hire a sitter and take Granny too. Couldn't she sit and watch?"

"Sure," said Kate.

Granny pushed herself out of her chair. "I better go take a nap," she said in a flutter.

Torrey talked all the way to the city with Dave. She learned that her father was still too angry to discuss her with anyone.

"I've tried," Dave told her, "and of course Mom's tried. He just clams up. Mom says to let things ride. You seem happy here. What do you hear from Cleve?"

Torrey told him. "One minute I think everything's all right, Dave, but the next I'm a bundle of doubts.

148

I'm not even sure then that Cleve loves me. Sometimes I think I don't even love him. Not enough, anyway. Not enough to go off down there and marry someone I don't seem to feel perfectly sure about."

"Love's a funny thing," said Dave. "You think you have it pinned down, and you don't at all. Like me and Jennie. I was almost sure it was love. Almost. Then I met Biddy."

"But, Dave—Biddy's just a child."

"She is now. But she's growing up so fast you can almost hear it." He smiled shyly at Torrey. "When the time comes I want to be around."

"How about Jennie?"

"She's dated George Webb once or twice. They'd make a much better team. Jennie's a farm girl. She needs a farmer."

"Aren't you a farmer?"

"Yes and no. I'm going to learn better ways to do it than Dad uses. I'll want things mechanized so's to free my hands. There are big things coming, Torrey. It doesn't make sense to work as hard as Dad does and never catch up."

That evening Dave and Nora and Kate and Granny waited for Biddy, parked by the drive-in. Torrey thought Biddy looked neat and attractive flying in and out in her maroon slacks and jaunty cap. At eight o'clock, when Biddy joined them, Torrey got out to let her sit next to Dave.

"Why didn't somebody tell me that having a job depends on your feet and not on your head?" Biddy sat back with a sigh of relief. Then she twisted around. "Hi, Granny! You look like Cinderella in that spangled scarf. You haven't had a night out for a long time. Where's Dennis?"

"He said he'd baby-sit if we paid him what we paid a sitter," answered Dave. "He and I settled it between us."

"Well, nobody ever did that for me!" sputtered Biddy.

"Maybe you never gave up anything to earn it."

"You haven't any idea of the things I've given up in my life, David Thorne. I'm a living sacrifice."

"I'll bet!"

"Are you a real good dancer?" she asked him.

"Passable. How're you?"

"I only know the ones everyone knows, and some Irish jigs. Up here they do real fancy stuff. Authentic foreign ones. Kolos and things. Last time they had a leader who taught us some Israeli dances."

"Fun?"

"Not exactly fun. The music was terribly sad. It tore you up in little bits. The steps were slow—and— I don't know—sort of *tortured*. But still you were glad to be doing it. You wanted to understand it."

Torrey was quiet. She was thinking about Dave and Biddy. It was true Biddy was young. An irresponsible, sassy adolescent most of the time. But she had Kate's warm impulsiveness and a lot of Nora's womanliness. She's a doer, thought Torrey. Biddy'd get Dave where he needed to go, and she'd get what she wanted from life, for herself and Dave and all their children. When Torrey thought of Biddy's children, she smiled to herself. Biddy'd probably paint all of their toenails green.

150

The folk dancing was in full swing in the open pavilion at Wolf Ridge. They found a place for Granny out of a draft. Sets were forming for a square dance.

Dave took Biddy with him. Kate and Nora entered the same set and found partners. As the men saw that these newcomers could hold their own in the faster dances, they had plenty of partners.

"Having fun, Granny?" asked Torrey as she dropped into a chair, hot and panting, after a lively circle dance.

"I am that. But I wish I could show 'em how to dance an Irish reel." Her toes were tapping.

"Don't you dare," cautioned Nora.

"Biddy can," said Granny. "I taught her myself years ago."

Torrey walked over to the caller, a thick-set woman in a beautifully worked Czech costume and flat ballet slippers. Her sturdy legs were bare.

"Hi, Torrey! Haven't seen you for ages. Where's that good-looking guy you came dancing with last spring?"

"Cavorting with beautiful señoritas in Santiago, Chile. Say, Felicia, any man here who can do an Irish jig or a reel? We've brought an old lady with us. She's over ninety. She hasn't seen one for years. Her great-granddaughter can do it, but she needs a partner."

"We'll soon find out." Felicia stepped to the microphone. "Here's a call for an Irish dance. We need a man. Whee! Here's Pat O'Flaherty, no less. The top of the evening to you, Pat. Got some Irish music

151

over there, Toni? Now where's this lass from Erin? Come along, don't be bashful."

Biddy didn't have to be asked twice.

"If there is one thing Biddy isn't, it's bashful," said Nora.

"Can you see them, Granny?" shouted Kate.

Granny nodded. "She's pretty, Biddy is. Almost as pretty as I was, if I do say so as shouldn't, an' why shouldn't I?"

Biddy and Pat O'Flaherty stepped off the dance with spirit. There was a burst of applause as they came to a laughing finish.

"You can dance like nobody's business, Biddy O'Shea," said Pat O'Flaherty.

"The same to yourself, an' the Lord love you," answered Biddy.

"An' can I have the next dance with you then?"

Biddy's violet eyes slid around to Dave. "Sure an' who's to stop us?"

From then on until midnight Dave had a hard time claiming Biddy for any dance.

On the way home she asked, "Did you care if I danced with Pat, Dave?"

"Why should I?"

"You shouldn't. But I'd feel a little safer about you if I thought you did."

"Biddy!" scolded Nora.

"If Dave isn't jealous, I'm heartbroken."

"Too bad," said Dave.

"When we get home I'll make you some hot chocolate. The way to a man's heart is—"

"If we're getting up at five," Dave answered, "we'd better hit the hay."

"Five!" Biddy's voice was anguished. "My feet won't even have feeling in them by five."

"Want to call it off?"

"Don't be facetious."

They didn't get away as soon as they expected. Nora begged off. "I'm so far behind. And I'd better keep an eye on Granny. She had a restless night. That was quite a jaunt for her. And if I keep the little ones here, you'll only need one car."

The morning was cool and fresh. They drove up to the Skyline and along the Crystal Lakes. There was a filmy mist over the silver water. The oaks formed a wooded backdrop, and the road was bordered with teazel, with here and there the blue flowers of flax.

"Granny says this is like parts of Ireland," said Kate. "And the MacPhersons say it's like the Scottish lochs in the Ben Lomond country."

It wasn't long before they saw the glint of the ocean, like a sheet of polished steel below them. On one side of the road were commercial flower beds, dewy and cool in the early light. Rows of pinky-lavender heather marched up the low hills. Purple, pink, and white stock bloomed in even rows. Frothy fields of artichokes sat cheek by jowl with rows and rows of pink geraniums.

They drove north to Montara, where the long beach stretched away to a rocky promontory. The valley behind it dreamed in the morning sun.

They found a sheltered spot at the foot of the cliffs, where Dave built a small fire. The waves came rolling in, a clear translucent green, to topple and crash into roaring foam that slid in sheets of white

153

up the beach, leaving fringes of iridescent bubbles on the sand.

They ate Mom's fried chicken and potato salad and cheese rolls and cake as easily at six-thirty as they would have at noon.

"I don't know why we don't do this more often," said Kate. "It's heavenly."

They watched the gulls and the tiny sandpipers feeding along the edge of the waves. They walked along the wet sand, finding queer water-worn rocks, shells, gray driftwood, sprays of sea moss. They climbed the rocks where pools of water reflected the blue sky.

When the sun had warmed them, they retired one by one to a sheltered cove and appeared in bathing suits. No one felt like a swim, the water was too cold. They raced into the ocean, jumped the breakers, and came gasping out again.

It did something for Torrey. She had forgotten the library board meeting and Miss Cluney Mary. She was remembering Cleve and that heavenly day at the beach when he had slid the big diamond on her hand, all gritty with sand. Cleve liked this kind of thing, she was thinking. Half our dates were beach parties. And he chose to tell me he loved me with the wind in our faces and the sound of the surf in our ears. Let him dance, down there in Santiago. He will remember waves breaking on an ocean beach and sand between his toes.

They got Biddy back to the drive-in in time and drove up to Nora's relaxed and happy, to find the doctor's car in front of the house.

"It's Granny," said Nora, her face drawn and worried.

"Bad?" Kate asked.

"We don't know. It's hard to tell. The doctor says anything can happen at ninety-five."

Dave said good-bye and started back. Torrey took the three little ones out to her own room.

Dennis came wandering out there after a bit, his face so white his freckles stood out one by one. "I just can't stand it, Torrey, to have Granny dy-dying." He turned away, staring across the waving grain of the seminary. "First my father gone, and now Granny."

"But you were too young, Dennis. You weren't even born."

"I don't mean him. I mean Bob. He's such a swell guy, Torrey, and he's been gone such a long time."

Torrey opened up a box of Mom's cookies. She heated milk and made some hot chocolate. "Everybody sit on the bed but Dennis. He can have the chair."

It's funny, she was thinking as she watched him tuck in the cookies, for feast and frolic, in sorrow and grief, food plays such an important part.

Another car stopped. Torrey tried to stand between Dennis and the window as she watched a priest hurry up the ramp that had been built in place of steps for Granny's wheelchair.

"They ought to send for Biddy," Dennis said at her shoulder. "Biddy's Granny's own."

"Go over quietly and speak to Nora, Dennis. Ask her if you should go down for Biddy."

But at that moment Biddy came running up the

walk. At sight of her brother's stricken face at the window, she veered off to Torrey's room.

"She's dying," faltered Dennis. "Oh, Biddy! Granny's dying."

Biddy nodded. "Mom phoned the drive-in."

"You shouldn't have taken her out last night," said Dennis.

"I'm glad we did," Biddy told him fiercely. "I'm glad as anything. Granny had one last fling." She put her arm across his shoulder. "Don't you cry, Dennis. Here's my handkerchief. Granny's been willing to go for a long time. I think the Lord's going to be very pleased to get somebody like Granny."

16

TORREY did what she thought would be most use-
ful. She kept the three youngest with her, sending over for their sleepers and slippers and bath-
robes, getting them bathed and fed. She and Kate
carried them back to bed, and Torrey told them
stories and sang Mother Goose songs, until all three
were safely off to sleep.

As she came out of their room, she met Biddy in the
hall. Biddy was weeping. Torrey gathered her into
her arms, much as she had gathered up small
Molly. "She's an old, tired lady, Biddy. Don't grieve
for her."

Biddy twisted away. "I'm not grieving for Granny.
I'm weeping bitter tears for my own witless, gatless
self. The spirit of prophecy was on you, Torrey
Thorne, when you said I must get Granny's stories
down before it was too late. Granny's gone. It's too
late now. I'll never, never forgive myself, all the
days of my years and the years of my life."

"The stories will come back to you, Biddy, when

157

you want them. And when they do, they won't be Granny's stories any longer. They'll be the stories of Biddy O'Shea."

But Biddy wouldn't listen.

At the Requiem Mass, Torrey was surprised to see Miss Cluney Mary.

"I didn't know you were staying with my old friend," said Miss Cluney Mary. "I had no idea that Biddy was her great-grandchild. I have known Granny all my life. I went to the convent with her daughter."

"This whole family is going to miss her," said Torrey.

"Yes. She was a great lady. I have been meaning to drop in and see her for a long time. But . . ." her voice trailed off, "where does the time go?"

Torrey looked at her watch. "There will be hordes of people at Nora's. I must keep the children from under foot. I have to be at the library at one."

"Come and see me, Miss Thorne." But Torrey was gone. She did not see the hand that Miss Cluney Mary had put out.

Nothing was said about the library board meeting. Looks like I still have a job, thought Torrey. All that worry for nothing. In all the confusion she had almost forgotten the story hour at Las Pulgas. At three o'clock she cleared her desk and went in to get her purse. Life goes on, she thought.

She poked her head in to Mr. Brock's office. "Do I pick up the station wagon in the parking lot?"

"No, it's at the garage. I've told them you were to take it. Do you know how to get to the branch?"

"I looked it up on the map. I've given myself extra time to get lost."

He laughed. "Stop and ask in the workroom if there's anything they'd like to send along. Requests or supplies are always waiting to go."

At Las Pulgas, Stella Stanley had a whole roomful of youngsters milling around, chattering like magpies. "It's a stampede," she said. "I can't count 'em until you get 'em quiet, but there's more than fifty, I betcha." She clapped her hands, and the buzz calmed down. "Here's the storyteller," she told them. "Where do you want them, Torrey?"

"I'll stand here," Torrey decided. "Most of you will have to sit on the floor. Settle down, everybody." She waited, her eyes seeking the eyes of the restless ones. She felt at ease, relaxed.

"All you need to bring to a story hour," she told them, "is a good pair of listening ears."

The children grinned and several put their hands to their ears and waggled them.

"Once upon a time," began Torrey, "there was a little girl who lived close to the edge—of a jungle."

The word "jungle" did it. She had them, then, under the spell of her voice. A roomful of children so absorbed that she could feel their concentration. It was a wonderful feeling, heady and inspiring. She drew laughter from them and laughed with them.

After "The Gunniwolf" she read them Allingham's poem, "The Fairies." It was too long for children unaccustomed to poetry. She had lost them. She cut it to three verses and plunged into "Peterkin and the Little Gray Hare."

Then they asked for stories they knew, and she

159

promised to tell one of them the next time. "You going to be here *again?*" they asked.

"She sure is," said Stella Stanley, "if you want her."

They shouted their approval and the few adults in the library laughed at the enthusiasm.

"Wouldn't mind coming myself," said an old man crowded into a corner trying to read a newspaper.

"Come along," said Torrey, "there's room for everybody."

"There must have been seventy-five here," said Stella Stanley. "We'll have to hire a hall."

Torrey stayed to help stamp out books and hand out the applications for cards. It was five-thirty before she left, and she still had to take the station wagon back to the garage downtown. She reached home tired out.

"Have dinner with us, Torrey," urged Nora. "Everybody in town's been here with food."

It was good for Nora and Kate and Dennis—and most of all Biddy—to have Torrey at this first meal without Granny. She told them about the story hour and how the children had laughed at Peterkin.

"Is it hard to learn to tell stories?" asked Biddy.

"Not if you learn them in patterns, in a series of pictures in your mind."

"Does it take a long time?"

"It isn't easy. But you start with simple ones."

"I'd like to learn. Maybe I could learn to tell stories like—" Biddy's voice choked up.

"I'll help you."

"It's a deal," said Biddy thickly.

At the end of the week Torrey got her first pay-check and was bitterly disappointed. After all the deductions there was less than a hundred and thirty dollars. She could see now that Mom had been right. There wouldn't be much left over for the hope chest. By the time she had paid room rent, laundry, and part of what she owed Dave, she'd have a hard time paying for groceries for a month.

She would have college expenses in a few weeks, tuition and transportation and books, and the dozens of little, incidental expenses that had somehow grown so much bigger than they used to be.

"I'll make it if I starve," she told herself fiercely.

Each week Torrey went early to Las Pulgas. She straightened out the picture books and left some of her pet books, like *Caddie Woodlawn* and *Johnny Tremain* on the book truck.

"They think they've just been circulated," said Stella Stanley, "so they must be good."

Torrey helped set up the chairs and pushed back the tables to make room for the growing crowd of children.

"You don't have to do that," protested Stella Stanley. "Come and have a cup of tea."

"I know I don't, but, Stella, you have too much to do. I don't mind. There's a wonderful atmosphere in this library."

"Yes. They make themselves at home, all right."

Dad had been right. Torrey was putting far more than half-time into her job. It was impossible to learn stories on library time. There were too many interruptions. Often it was necessary to take extra time to find her stories. She took home armloads of books, both new children's books she needed to know and story material. She propped herself up on her

161

bed, read and reread her stories, and then told them out loud to herself. She tried them out at bedtime on Pat and Mike and small Molly.

Up in the hills beyond the Las Pulgas branch there was a small, closely knit colony of Portuguese people. Torrey could pick out the children in her audience by their rounded, smooth brown cheeks and big brown eyes.

After one story hour one of these youngsters asked her, "Next time you come, will you tell us a Portuguese story?"

Torrey was delighted. It pleased her to have this dark-eyed boy proud of his racial heritage. "Yes, if I can find one," she told him.

It wasn't easy. She could find collections of Norse stories, Albanian, Russian, Greek, almost anything but Portuguese. She hunted until she found one that she liked. It needed cutting and pruning, but Torrey felt that she had found a story good enough to add to her growing repertoire of tales to tell. It was the Portuguese version of "The Twelve Dancing Princesses."

Torrey found herself looking forward to Tuesdays. Many of the mothers came now, to sit on the edge of a table and then to gather up books and children when the stories were over. They stopped to talk over books for their children, and Torrey prepared lists for them and brought up special books for them to see. Natalie Lennox, the P.T.A. President for the school near the library, asked her to talk to her group. Torrey chose for her title, "As the Twig Is Bent."

She began to take home books that told about

stories, as well as the stories themselves. Some of these she had used in Dr. Jordan's class, like Marie Shedlock's *The Art of the Storyteller* and Ruth Sawyer's *The Way of the Storyteller*. Some of them she dug up for herself in the adult section of the library, books on folklore, on Indian gods, on superstitions, and collections of Oriental stories.

She began to learn Irish stories, trying to remember Granny's phrases and the turn of the sentences that stamped the stories as Irish as soon as she opened her mouth.

She tried an Uncle Remus story but found it difficult. "Why doesn't it sound right?" she complained to Clarissa.

"You don't have the proper lilt to it. Listen. 'Tar baby ain't sayin' nothin', an' Br'er Fox, he lay low.' The 'lay' is high, and the 'low' is *low*."

"Think I'll ever get it?"

"Yes, if you want to. Listen to some of these children who come in here. There's a cadence—"

Cleve wrote in answer to Torrey's long letter, "I'm sorry about the ring and Gang and your dad. I wish I were there. I think I could get them to see the light. Keep on trying, Torrey, to understand Gang. She's really a wonderful person. But I know she can be difficult too." He ended his letter with: "It's our life, Torrey, and from here on out no one else can decide things for us."

Torrey read this over and over.

Did Cleve really mean it? She remembered Mona's words, "People like Cluney Mary can't stand being stood up to." Would Cleve stand up to Miss Cluney Mary Clevinger the way his letter sounded?

163

Dave came over every few weeks, loaded down with Mom's good cooking. They all went over to the beach or to Butano Forest or down the coast to Santa Cruz.

Some Sundays Torrey went to her own church, while Nora and Kate took their family to Mass. Torrey could see Miss Cluney Mary sitting alone in all her glory in a front pew. She bowed distantly to Torrey as she swept out to greet the minister.

As Torrey hurried home to learn stories, she was thinking to herself that this churchgoing by herself was a lonely business.

Biddy was quieter since Granny's death. She certainly wasn't as scatterbrained as she had been. She kept her job at the drive-in, and she and Dennis pooled their funds, determined to get the dishwasher for Nora.

"It's as much for Dennis and me as it is for Mom," Biddy explained. "It's to save my dishpan hands. Will you like me better then, David Thorne?"

"I'll make a special effort," he answered.

The summer vacation drew to a close. The grain was gold now in the field beneath the oak trees.

Torrey was at peace with her world as long as she kept her mind on it and didn't think too much about Cleve. Her only social life was the fun with Nora's family and an occasional movie with Clarissa. She was happy when Dave came, and she watched him and Biddy with amusement and some concern. She didn't want either of them hurt.

She felt unhappy about her dad, but she figured that there was nothing she could do about that situation at present.

And then, just before it was time for Kate to go off to Belvedere and for Torrey to start her own classes at college, a special letter came from Cleve.

Does the road wind up-hill all the way?
Yes, to the very end

CHRISTINA ROSSETTI—UP-HILL

17

IT LOOKED LIKE ALL THE OTHER LETTERS she had received, with the Chilean stamps marked Correo *Aereo Chile* and Cleve's familiar scrawl on the outside. But inside there was a draft for five hundred dollars. His letter told her that he had found an apartment for them and that he wanted her to come —now.

"I need you, Torrey. Let's not waste this whole year. Get a ticket and come, just as you are. Tell them all to jump in the lake, Gang and your dad and everybody. It's our life, ours together. We'll have fun down here. These people aren't bad. I've learned to like them. They'll fall for you just like I did, hook, line, and sinker. Wire me collect, 'I'm coming,' and tell me when, so I won't go crazy waiting for you."

Torrey put the draft in her desk and the letter back in the long envelope. She wrapped a white stole about her shoulders and tucked the letter in the pocket of her dress. Then she walked out of her room and down the drive. Turning her face to the setting sun, she started up the long hill across from the ivy-covered stone wall.

For a long time she walked without much thought, under liquid amber maples just beginning to turn. A few cars passed. There were children playing at some of the houses. One of them called out to her, "Hi, Story Lady!" and Torrey waved, "Hi!"

Cleve, she was thinking. Cleve and I in Santiago, Chile. Me with my well-worn clothes. No linen, no silver, no pots and pans. Just Torrey Thorne, on Cleve Macklin's money. What would the Chileño friends of Cleve Macklin think of her, arriving shabby and penniless in Santiago? Without the blessing of her own family or his? Cleve, Cleve! Darling, I can't!

Then she felt the letter in her pocket and pulled it out to read again. "I need you, Torrey."

Pioneer women didn't stop for what people would think. They packed up what they had, babies too, if they were married, and came West when their men sent for them. She thought of one great-grandmother three years younger than Torrey herself, who had come with two small children over the fearful, fever-ridden trail across the Isthmus as soon as her young husband had sent the gold dust to make it possible.

But Torrey Thorne wouldn't be going to a pioneer country as a married woman. She would be entering a well-established society where there were certain social taboos. Would they understand her position and Cleve's? Would they condone it? What would she think of some girl who let a man pay her way to

167

South America to marry him? I'd have to know all the facts, she admitted. And how could we tell people the facts? We couldn't. They'd just guess, and some of the guessing would be tolerant, and some of it wouldn't.

Some of the criticism would be aimed at Cleve; most of it would be directed at her and her family.

Or were people more willing to accept a situation like that now? Was she being Victorian? Weren't people flying around the world for all sorts of reasons? Wasn't life everywhere more fluid, less hidebound? Hadn't Miss Cluney Mary said that this South American friend who had spirited Cleve away with him was dynamic? Wouldn't dynamic people accept a girl like Torrey Thorne for what she was and not for what it looked like?

She was remembering Dr. Jordan's estimate of her. "You have youth, personality, breeding, a certain amount of pulchritude—"

Would the friends Cleve had made in Santiago, Chile, see beyond the certain amount of pulchritude to the breeding?

She plodded on up the hill, not thinking now. Letting the soft evening breeze cool her flushed face. Walking, walking, walking, hugging the thin jersey stole around her shoulders, not because she was cold but because she needed something to hug about her.

A long black car slid to the curb. As Torrey looked up the window of the back seat was lowered. "Miss Thorne! How nice to run across you like this!"

Torrey walked over to the car. "Good evening, Miss Clevinger."

"May we take you wherever you are going?"

Torrey smiled. She was well past the houses and the golf course, even beyond the grazing fields of the stables. The only other home ahead was the Clevinger house. "Thank you. I'm walking. I had no idea I had come so far. I—I had some things to think out. I just kept going."

"Get in. I'll take you up to the house, and we can have a bite to eat together. Honniger will take you home. It will be dark before you get back. This is a lonely road after dark."

Torrey would rather have been left alone. But wasn't this a chance to be on better terms with Miss Cluney Mary? Cleve had asked her to be friendly. She got in and sat beside Miss Clevinger.

"Do you often walk out like this, Miss Thorne—Torrey, isn't it?"

"Yes, it's Torrey, and I like to walk, but I seldom find the time. I seem to spend most of my time learning stories."

"Yes. I have heard about your stories. At Las Pulgas. The mothers of our small fry up here are very much pleased with your stories and your work with the children."

"How nice of you to tell me. I enjoy the children. It's fun to learn new stories for them. And they are beginning to enjoy poetry. At first I couldn't hold their attention."

"I always loved it."

"I did too. I have a hard time finding worthwhile things that are simple enough for them, things that I like myself."

"A. A. Milne? I used to read him to Clevinger."

169

"Only a few of his yet. Although they are beginning to be more enthusiastic about things—just because I am."

"And Mother Goose? Do people still read Mother Goose? When I hear some of these quiz programs, I wonder if they do."

"We do. We say them together."

"Good!"

They were served a fruit salad out by the swimming pool. Torrey enjoyed the fruit, but she wished she could have had a hand in the dressing. But it didn't matter. She could look across the pool and down over the soft, brown, oak-dotted hills to where the lights of the cities along the bay were beginning to gleam. A single star glittered and pulsed in the pale sky. Wish I may, wish I might, Torrey was thinking.

"Have you heard recently from Clevinger—eh—Torrey?"

"Yes." On a sudden impulse Torrey leaned forward. "Miss Clevinger, Cleve has asked me again to join him in Santiago and marry him there."

Miss Cluney Mary put down her glass of iced tea. Her face was still. Torrey could not tell how she felt. "And you are going?"

"No."

There was a pause. Is she glad? wondered Torrey. Is she sorry for me?

"I think you are very wise. You know, Miss Thorne, I have changed my mind a little about you and Clevinger."

Torrey sat still, wondering what was coming.

The woman at the small table across from her was

170

looking down at the rolling hills and the gleaming lights. "Don't misunderstand me," she said a little harshly. "I am not discussing the suitability of this affair."

Torrey flared up at this. "It has never been an affair, Miss Clevinger. It has been an engagement in good faith. I am sorry if you feel that I am not suitable for Cleve."

Miss Cluney Mary put up an impatient hand. "I haven't said that. I feel that you are not suitable for each other."

"Well, my father feels the same way about it. I have had to leave home because he is so angry at my getting engaged to a man who did not come to him first. I think that you and my father have the viewpoint of another generation. It is hard for us to understand each other."

"Perhaps. But I think that after twenty years I have some claim to understanding Clevinger. More so, I think, than you could have after a few weeks."

Torrey nodded. "That is the reason I am not going to South America. When I get married I must be very sure that I am doing the thing that is best for me and for Cleve and for our families. Both my own and you and the family we hope to have."

"I have had two very indignant letters from my boy, about his mother's ring. You must have written him."

"Yes. I wrote soon after I heard from Cleve. About you and the ring and my father. I tried to be fair to both of us—to all of us."

"Would you like it back?"

Torrey was taken off guard by this question.

Would she? Mom would want her to have it because somehow it saved face for Torrey. Cleve wanted her to have it because he had given it to her with all his love. She thought of the day she had watched the story hour class in the facets of the large diamond. She saw it again in that last bitter twinkle of Miss Clevinger's hand as she disappeared so smoothly up the stairway. No. Right now she never wanted to see it again. There was too much heartbreak wrapped up in the ring.

"I don't think so," she answered slowly. "Cleve and I do not need a symbol." She rose and stood on the edge of the shimmering turquoise pool. "I must be getting back. I have found an interesting South American story and I must get it learned."

"I will call Honniger."

"Thank you." Torrey felt too tired to take the long walk home in the dusk.

As they waited for the car, Miss Cluney Mary was saying, "I find Biddy O'Shea very refreshing. She is quite lovely, isn't she? She has her great-grand-mother's early beauty. Where does she go to school?"

"Marysdale High School. Biddy's darling. I have enjoyed her and her family. They have made me feel very welcome. Biddy has real talent."

"I am glad to hear that. The one I knew so well was her grandmother. Kitty O'Hare could have been a great actress. But it would have been unthinkabl[e] for a young girl of that era, in her social position, t[o] appear upon the stage."

Torrey was indignant. "I don't see why. That mu[st] have been about Maude Adams' time."

"Miss Adams was the exception that proves th[e]

rule. Here in California the old families held very definite views on the subject."

"What do you mean by 'old families,' Miss Clevinger?" Why do I argue with her? Torrey asked herself. We'll never get together on this sort of thing.

"People who have been here for several generations, Miss Thorne. They are thinning out now. Most of the people on the Peninsula are newcomers. I feel that it has meant a lowering of standards."

"You think the standards during the Gold Rush were high? Or did the standards climb as people made money?"

"All kinds of people came in the Gold Rush," admitted Miss Clevinger, "but—"

" 'Scoundrels from nowhere,' " quoted Torrey.

"They weren't all scoundrels, I am sure, Miss Thorne." There was an edge to Miss Clevinger's voice.

"Of course not," Torrey agreed. Then she added with wicked relish, "All eight of my grandparents came at that time. I'm sure they couldn't *all* have been scoundrels."

The big black car drew up into the parking place below the pool. "Thank you, Miss Clevinger, for the supper and for the lift home."

"I hope now that you have found your way here, Miss Thorne, you will come again. Walk up some evening, and we'll see that you get safely back."

"Thank you. But I have settled my weighty problem. I will write Cleve tonight that I will not be coming down to Chile." Her voice trailed off forlornly.

"You love him very much, don't you?"

Don't wear your heart on your sleeve, Torrey Thorne, she told herself, for this jackdaw to peck at. But she found herself saying simply, "With all my heart."

Torrey wrote and rewrote her letter to Cleve that night. Then she added the five-hundred-dollar draft, sealed it and walked down the street to mail it. She felt she must get it safely on its way, before she could change her mind.

A week later she signed up for two classes at college in storytelling and children's literature. They were to be taught, the schedule told her, by a Mrs. Dixon.

But when Torrey walked in to the storytelling class, she came face to face with Dr. Carlson Jordan.

18

A T THE BREAK THAT AFTERNOON Mona was casting stitches on a round needle. "Look, Clarissa, I have them all cast on. What do I do next?"

"Knit, purl, knit, purl, three times around for an edge."

"Dress?" asked Torrey.

"Yes. I'm out of my mind. But Clarissa says if she can do it anybody can do it. She's going to chaperone me every inch of the way. Who's teaching your courses, Tor?"

"Jordan. He flunked me at Library School, and I walk in and there he is. Dixon broke a leg or something, so it's Jordan."

"Bother you?"

"Sure. If he flunks me this time, I'll commit something. But it's funny. He scared the wits out of me last year, but I learned a lot before I got sidetracked with man trouble. He knows stories and books and sources, and that's what I want. When he gets started on where stories came from, I forget all

175

about his conceited little bob and that eternal beard massage. He went into Sanskrit this morning, and the Ramayana. I can *see* what he's talking about. I'm fascinated."

"I think the wench is in love with him," murmured Mona. "Knit, purl, knit, purl."

"Heaven forbid!"

"Stranger things have happened. The darndest people fall for the darndest people."

"Have you ever been in love, Mona? Really in love, I mean?" asked Clarissa.

Torrey held her breath.

"Dozens of times. Every time I meet a new man my heart coos, 'This is *it*!' But there's been only one man in my life—" she stopped to push the knit stitches around the gleaming needle. "Think this idiot's delight will ever be a knitted dress?"

Torrey poured herself another cup of coffee. "Just one man?" she probed.

"Yep. Most of 'em, I can take 'em or leave 'em. But there's one, if I ever get a tumble from that guy, everybody better 'step aside.' "

Was it Cleve? Torrey hoped it wasn't. She liked Mona. She felt that Mona liked her. She hoped that the one man in Mona's life wouldn't turn out to be the one man in Torrey Thorne's life.

Torrey worked hard preparing stories for Dr. Jordan. Her experience in telling stories at Las Pulgas stood her in good stead. She was able to use them for his class, and he agreed to count her library stories for what he called 'clinic experience.'

But he drove her far harder than any of his oth-

176

pupils. He asked her to learn special stories, selections from the better children's books. He criticized her storytelling unmercifully.

At one session he interrupted her impatiently. "This is a love story you're telling us, Miss Thorne. All the Cinderella stories—and there are some three hundred and fifty known versions of that eternal story—are all love stories. But you don't make it sound like love. Love is like an egg—if there is any doubt about it, there is *no* doubt about it!"

How did you make a story sound like love? But Torrey tried.

Another time he growled irritably, "It would increase our enjoyment, Miss Thorne, if you sounded as though you yourself found this story amusing. Your words about Homer Price tell us he is supposed to be funny, but you don't look as though you thought so. There is no laughter in your voice. Make your audience see that machine grinding out a tidal wave of doughnuts. It's like 'The Sorcerer's Apprentice.' Something started that can't be stopped. McCloskey has caught it in his pictures. Get it into your story. And collect the eyes of your audience to share the joke with them."

"I was trying to collect my wits," Torrey answered ruefully, "It's the first time I've told it."

"Try it again on Friday." His voice was resigned. "Get some fun into it. Make your audience understand the joy of that middle-aged, overweight, too rich woman, as she turns, quite happily, to making those doughnuts. Emphasize, just a trifle, the fact that she strips off her jewelry. The way you told it I didn't remember anything about that, and yet it's the clue to the whole denouement. You have to tap on clues in storytelling exactly as you do in story writing."

Torrey tried it again on Friday, and Dr. Jordan gave it a grudging nod of approval. "May I see you after class, Miss Thorne?"

Torrey was remembering the day when he had asked the same thing of her, the day she had let a diamond ring come between her and her interest in stories or in anything but Cleve Macklin. The diamond was gone. Cleve was still—would always be—the most important thing in her life. But now she knew that no one person, no one thing, must be so important to her that Torrey Thorne should forget everything else. She knew now that everyone had certain disciplines, certain obligations to others, to oneself, that must be met.

Dr. Jordan rocked on his heels, stuck his thumbs in his vest pockets, and rattled his fingers on his tight paunch. Torrey saw all this and grinned to herself. It made him what he was, she decided. He was conceited, but then he had a certain right to be, the right of any great scholar to be himself. He was an authority in his own field, a teacher whose wealth of knowledge he shared effectively, if pompously, with his students.

"Miss Thorne," he was saying, "I am pleased with you."

Torrey waited while he teetered on his small feet and stroked his little pepper-and-salt beard. "I get along with my students when they work for me. The County Welfare people have asked me to produce a storyteller for the cerebral-palsied children at San Idlefonso. I'd like you to do it once a week, as a library service. Brock is willing. Will you try it?"

"I guess so."

"A new experience for you. Not easy. Start with the cumulative stories and work up. These children can take anything. They need stories. They need a contact with a person like yourself. Try it and see."

The first time Torrey tried it she felt certain she couldn't go back. I'll tell them I can't fit it into my full schedule, she told herself. I can't have my heart torn to shreds while I tell stories.

"Will you tell us the Tar Baby story next time?" asked one small boy, leaning forward against his three-legged crutches. "It's the funniest story I ever heard."

Torrey didn't have the heart to fail him. "Yes," she promised. It would be hard to learn, she knew that. But Clarissa would help her.

When Torrey got back to the library there was a call from Miss Cluney Mary. "I am giving a luncheon for a young friend of mine, Mona Kingsley. Just a small pre-debutante party, before the season gets under way."

I haven't a thing to wear, thought Torrey, and I won't know a soul.

"I would like to have you meet some of Clevinger's friends," Miss Cluney Mary was saying.

So they can see how nice I am? wondered Torrey. Or so I can see how much more suitable they are? "I'm not free on weekdays, Miss Clevinger."

179

"This is a week from Saturday. May I count on you?"

Torrey felt trapped. "Thank you very much."

Mona Kingsley, she was thinking, as she hung up. Good heavens! That was Mona! Not some strange debutante at Woodside or Hillsborough or Burlingame. This was Mona, reference librarian at the Marysdale Library. Mona with the etched face and caustic comments who liked people and books enough to work in a library when she didn't have to. Torrey was hearing Clarissa the day they talked about Mona. Mona and Cleve. Torrey winced when she thought of that. "And he took Mona out a lot, partying and skiing and folk dancing."

Now Miss Cluney Mary was having a luncheon for Mona, and Torrey Thorne was invited. Why? So they can see what a nice girl Clevinger Macklin had chosen for his future wife? Torrey doubted that. Or so we can see how unsuitable we are for each other. That was more like it.

Torrey thought of her worn wardrobe. I'm not going to buy clothes until I get Dave paid back, she told herself. She felt like Cinderella, with no fairy godmother to clothe her, to shoe her in fragile glass. No golden coach. She'd have to hire a taxi out of her own slim funds to get there. And no prince to dance with when she faced the music.

Why didn't I keep my head and find a way out of this? I could have said I was going to Belvedere, and then go. I don't want to meet these girls. No, that's not true. I like Mona and maybe I'll like the rest of them. But will they like me?

She wished again that she hadn't accepted.

180

Biddy talked with Torrey whenever she had a chance. "Dave says he doesn't care if I go to dances and things," she explained carefully. "He says I can't be a *recluse*. I don't tell people how it is. I don't have his pin or anything. But I have his flashlight. I sleep with it under my pillow."

Torrey remembered the oily work glove with the thumb missing which she had treasured for months when she thought she was in love with the boy who drove the tractor at the ranch one summer. "It's all right, Biddy, as long as you keep your sense of proportion."

Biddy grinned. "I haven't much sense," she admitted, "but my proportions are excellent. I only wish I had something to clothe them in. Here's the Frolic coming up, and all I have to wear is that old blue rag I've worn for two solid years. It's as tattered as an old flag whipped in a high breeze."

"Haven't you saved any of the money you've earned?"

"Yep, most of it. But Dennis is catching up with his half, and then we're going to get the dishwasher. We thought we had the money all earned, but we forgot the tax."

Torrey remembered what Kate had said back at college. "All I can think of now is that I can get Biddy a new formal."

But Kate hadn't earned her first paycheck yet. And Torrey knew that funeral expenses had strained Nora's slim finances to the limit. Granny's pension was gone too. She wished she could help, but that was hopeless.

"It's tough," she admitted. "If it will make you

181

feel any better, I'm in the same boat. Miss Cluney Mary has invited me to a luncheon, and I haven't a decent thing to wear."

"Torrey!" Biddy forgot her own problem. "You *have* to be beautiful, on account of to put that old girl's eye out."

"If wishes were horses—"

"I really don't have to worry," said Biddy, "because the blue flutter is plenty good enough for the Frolic. And Dave would go right on loving me if I turned up in a gunnysack."

"I don't think—" Torrey meant to say that Dave wasn't as safely Biddy's as that young lady seemed to feel. But why should she? Let Biddy dream. Especially since she didn't have a new formal.

"But you really need clothes, Torrey, to meet those people. Looney Mary is diabolic. She's a weaving spider-woman. She likes to sit back and watch her victims struggle. She—"

"Oh, Biddy! Don't be such a goon. She's critical of me, of course. A perfectly strange girl walking off with the boy who has been like a son to her. She just wants to know me better."

"Don't get illusions of grandeur. She'd gladly poison your stuffed avocado. The woman's a Borgia and she means to stop you cold. She couldn't do it by taking your ring or by sending Cleve out of the country. So she's going to show you up in front of everybody."

Torrey sighed, afraid Biddy might be right. But she still didn't know what to do about it. By scrimping and scraping she had managed to bank a little each payday for the hope chest. But she had paid Dave only half of what she owed him. "I can't help it, Biddy. When you haven't got the money—" she shrugged.

Later Biddy came over again with a handful of mail.

There was a letter from Cleve. Torrey opened it to scan Cleve's disappointed words. He had received the draft and her letter. He was heartsick because she had decided not to come. "Why?" he demanded. "Is it Gang? I'll write her a real sizzler. I'm not going to let anyone come between us, now or ever."

"I got a letter too," said Biddy. "From New York. I can't imagine—Yipes! It's a check!" Biddy was spinning around like a top. "A check for thirty-five dollars. It says right on it 'Biddy O'Shea.'"

"Where from?" Torrey was almost as excited as Biddy.

Biddy began to read the letter. It was in the form of a contract from a juvenile magazine. It said that a story called "Paddy and the Green Goat" had been accepted for publication in the March issue. It said a lot more, but that was as far as Biddy got.

"Where did they ever get it?" She clutched the letter to her throat.

"I sent it," admitted Torrey. "I'd forgotten all about it. Do you care?"

"Care! I'd never have sent it anywhere. I wouldn't know where to. Thirty-five dollars. Look, Torrey! Wouldn't that be enough to buy you a dress to put Looney Mary's eye out?"

"It isn't going to. It's going to buy Biddy O'Shea

183

the prettiest formal at the Stanford Shopping Center."

"I think you should have some of it, Torrey. I'd never have sent it anywhere."

"I didn't write it. All I did was to type it up and send it off. Ages ago."

"A story of mine in a magazine!" Biddy's voice was full of awe. "Printed in black and white. I wish Granny were here. It's her story, really."

"I bet Granny knew, when she told you all those stories, that you'd use them someday."

"Won't the kids at school be ever bowled over! Wish Mom would come home. I have lots more stories. Shall I send them too?"

"Sure. Strike while the iron's hot."

"Will David Thorne be proud of me?"

"He'll bust all his buttons."

Biddy skipped to the door. "If I bring you some of them, will you type them for me?"

Torrey's heart sank. She still had two stories to learn for this week. Then she remembered Biddy's generous offer: "Look, Torrey! Wouldn't it be enough to buy you a dress to put Looney Mary's eye out?" "Sure," she answered. "But you'd better learn to type things up for yourself. I won't be here forever."

"If I sold a story a month—"

"Don't begin counting chickens before they're laid. It's a rough, tough game—" But Biddy was gone.

Torrey was left alone to worry about clothes for Miss Cluney Mary Clevinger's luncheon for Mona Kingsley.

19

Torrey pulled her soiled white gloves over her hands and scrubbed them in warm, soapy water. She rolled them in a towel, pulled them into shape, and spread them out to dry. She went over her mustard wool for spots and polished the cherry red belt and sandals.

"There!" she said aloud, "I'm ready for the party."

She had said nothing to Mona about the invitation. She seldom saw her at the library without someone else there, and Torrey hesitated to discuss a party to which only the two of them had been invited.

If Torrey felt a little shy with Mona since she had heard that Mona and Cleve had known each other so well, it was her own fault. Mona was as brusque and as friendly as she had always been.

The day before the luncheon, during the fifteen-minute coffee break, Mona knitted around the circular needle with a grim intensity.

"'S matter, Mona?" asked Clarissa. "You're tight as a fiddle string."

Mona put down her knitting and drained her cup. "I'm being hounded. I'm being pushed and driven along a groove I've never fitted. Square peg in a round hole."

"Who's pushing?" asked Clarissa.

"It's the same old hassle with my family. I've been swinging with both fists ever since I came home from school. I thought we had it all settled a year ago. I refused to go down the line. I came down here to the library to live my own life the way I like it." She poured another cup of coffee and set it down to cool. "Now the pressures are building up again. And you can't just shove people in the face when they want to be nice to you."

Torrey decided that Mona was talking about the coming debutante season. She wondered what it would be like. It always seemed so gay, so glamorous from the newspaper accounts. Bevies of lovely girls in exquisite gowns with their handsome, eligible young escorts.

And then some girl outside the magic circle, like Torrey Thorne, would come along and snatch up your eligible young man, because love was stronger than social mores. You could lead a young man like Cleve to the debutante line, but you couldn't force him to fall in love with one of them. Or had Cleve been in love with Mona? Had they quarreled, and then Cleve picked up the first pretty girl that pleased his fancy? Had Torrey Thorne caught Cleve Macklin on the rebound?

She wished she could banish these persistent

doubts that plagued her. She was hearing Dr. Jordan's voice, "Love is like an egg—if there is any doubt about it, there is *no* doubt about it."

Was her love for Cleve like that? Was there so much doubt about it there was no doubt about it?

"Snap out of it, Tor," said Mona. "You're worse than I am. You're in a blue fog. From the sounds of the trampling herd I think your room is full of pit ponies."

Torrey dressed for the luncheon on Saturday with mixed feelings. She was excited about having a luncheon date. Her work and lack of funds had tied her pretty closely to the library and to Nora's household. She hadn't had time to make friends. With Kate coming home most week ends and Dave coming up from the Valley, she hadn't felt the lack of dates.

But she was bothered too. Would they all be in cottons while she was in wool? What could she talk about to these girls whose lives were so different from her own? Did any of them know that Cleve Macklin had been dating her those last two months before he left for South America? Would they resent that? Would Mona, when she knew?

At the last minute, Torrey fastened around her neck the flat necklace of small, overlapping oak leaves that one great-grandmother had brought with her across the Isthmus. Only a little of it showed beneath the demure collar of the mustard dress. She put on the two matching oak-leaf earrings of onyx and gold that Mom had given her last Christmas after they had been converted from earrings

187

for pierced ears into clips. Somehow they gave Torrey courage.

She went over to Nora's to phone for a taxi.

"Don't do that," said Nora. "I'll call Anne. She'll drive you up. Then somebody up there can drive you back."

Whoever Anne was, she was glad to be obliging, but she'd have to wait until Carl could lift the seedlings she had just bought at the nursery out of the car. What was the deadline? Twelve-forty. Okay, Carl was due any minute.

When Torrey sat down in Nora's living room to wait, small Molly hurled herself onto her lap. She caught at Torrey's neck to hug her, and Torrey's hair was no longer its carefully arranged carelessness.

"Molly!" scolded Nora. "Don't get Torrey all mussed up. And your hands are dirty too!"

It was too late. There was a muddy smear across Torrey's cheekbone.

"Oh, Torrey, I'm so sorry," said Nora. "Here, you little devil, take your muddy self out of here and get cleaned up."

Molly howled at this injustice. "I just wanted to love her," she wailed.

Torrey went off to repair the damage. As she looked at herself in the bathroom mirror, she gave a nervous giggle. "Don't forget, Muddy Face, I love you," she whispered.

It was nearly one when Anne drove up. The back of her car was full of tall seedling trees in cans. "I'm beastly sorry. Carl hasn't come, and I prom ised I wouldn't lift these out by myself. Is it all right to go this way?"

"Sure," answered Torrey. What difference did it make? Nothing she did would make her anything but what she was, a poor but proud librarian, a country girl in old clothes, with no car, glad to get to her big date in anything on wheels.

Anne's car, with the seedlings whipping about, pulled up at the porte-cochere at the Clevinger house, and Torrey got out. The parking space beyond was glittering with long, sleek convertibles or small, compact sports cars.

When Torrey had thanked Anne, she picked up her red purse and her courage and walked up to the big door. It opened silently and Torrey murmured, "How are you, Mrs. Jones?"

Mrs. Jones, with set lips, was looking over Torrey's shoulder after the departing car and its waving seedlings.

Torrey was shown into a powder room. There were two other girls there. They glanced at Torrey, registered the fact that they didn't know her, said "Hi!" and went on talking.

It's like going to a strange house with a blind date, Torrey thought.

She walked out behind the girls into the big hexagonal library where Miss Cluney Mary, dressed in a brown ribbon knit, her white hair slicked back, stood before the black marble mantel.

"Miss Thorne, I want you to know some of my young friends. You know Mona, of course—you are both in the libr'ry."

"Hi, Tor," said Mona, and then under her breath,

"whyn't you tell me you'd be stuck with this? I'd have picked you up."

"Torrey Thorne!" A girl in a crisp navy linen came up.

Torrey had to think fast. "You're Natalie Lennox. From Las Pulgas."

"You're a whale of a success, gal, up there. We parents get a lot of fun out of listening. Your voice is lush."

Torrey laughed. "It works by itself. No brains."

"Come meet some of the girls who help with Little House."

Torrey forgot her wool dress. She forgot that she was a part-time librarian. Natalie Lennox was interested in what she was doing, not what she had on.

The luncheon was elegantly served at the long, inlaid table. As usual, it was tasteless. For the third time, Torrey was amazed at what a cook all dressed up in a high white cap could do to good food. She wondered if he had been watching the football games all morning.

Natalie Lennox sat next to Torrey, so there was no let-up in the flow of talk around her. A girl across the table called over, "Those earrings intrigue me. I can't help asking. Heirlooms?"

Torrey reached up and felt the smooth gold leaves with the onyx veins. "Yes. My great-grandmother brought them with her."

"You can always tell. We've some very much like them, but they're made for pierced ears."

"My mother had these converted."

"It's an idea."

Miss Cluney Mary sat at the head of the long

table, cool and gracious, a little removed from all the chatter. Torrey felt her deep-set, brown eyes looking down her way every so often. Was it as a considerate hostess who might be watching after the comfort of her guest, waiting to gather her into a general conversation if she seemed ill at ease? Was Miss Cluney Mary interested to note that Torrey Thorne had fitted into this group easily? Was she satisfied that the girl whom Cleve wanted to marry could meet and talk with the girls Miss Cluney Mary would have preferred? Was she interested in the heirlooms at Torrey's ears and throat? Or was her mind made up, set in the pattern of thought that Torrey Thorne and Cleve Macklin were not and never would be suitable for each other?

There was no way of telling.

But Miss Cluney Mary had invited Torrey Thorne to this luncheon. She didn't have to do that. She could have had this party for Mona without that, and Torrey would have read of it in the society pages of the paper. It would have hurt her badly. She would have thought of these girls very differently, hating them for their leisure, their self-assurance, their money. It would have come between her and Mona at the library.

"Tell them about your fan mail yesterday, Tor," said Mona.

Torrey realized she had been thinking to herself too long. At luncheons you didn't take time to think things through. You kept the ball rolling.

With her eyes crinkled up with laughter at herself, she said, "When I tell stories in the schools the teachers make the children write letters to thank

191

me. It kills two birds, manners and letter writing. But some of the spelling is fearful and wonderful. Yesterday one of the letters said, 'The minute you opened your mouth, a guiver went down my spin!'"

At the shout of laughter that went up, Miss Cluney Mary collected the eyes of her guests and rose from the table.

Mona drove Torrey home. "Awfully glad you were there, Tor. I hate shindigs like that. Uninteresting food and people you see all the time anyway."

"Thanks for the lift, Mona."

With her car purring softly, Mona leaned out of the window. "Mark my words, Tor. I'm going to get out of it. It isn't going to be easy, but I'm going to do it somehow. It isn't for me. I have to live my own life. I'm not going into that rat race. I'm going after what I want."

Because the road was steep and long
And through a dark and lonely land,
God . . . put a lantern in my hand

JOYCE KILMER—LOVE'S LANTERN

20

OCTOBER WAS A GOOD MONTH for stories. Torrey had an apple story hour, telling "Iduna and Her Golden Apples" and Pyle's "Apple of Contentment." She told ghost and witch stories for Hallowe'en and had the children bring in homemade masks. In no time patrons brought in all sorts of masks until Mona declared the place looked like a chamber of horrors.

The letters from Cleve had settled down to a sort of resignation. He wrote about the things he was doing, the people he was meeting. He made no further effort to persuade her to come down. It was three months since he had said good-bye from the airport.

Dave tried to talk Torrey into coming home for Thanksgiving. "Mom would love it. And I'm willing to bet as soon as you see Dad, he'll change his stubborn attitude. We can't really be thankful without you."

But Torrey, too, could be stubborn. "I'm not coming, Dave, until I can come with Cleve."

She and Kate helped Nora get Thanksgiving dinner. As she peeled and chopped, Torrey couldn't help being a little homesick. So many Thanksgivings she had done these things for Mom. She wondered if she would ever do them in her own home for Cleve.

"Set the table, Biddy," said Nora. "Torrey, do you want to arrange the fruit and vegetables any way you like for a centerpiece? I'll get this bird in the oven so we can get off to church. You going to church, Torrey?"

Torrey hadn't thought of going to church. She gave a little shiver. "No," she answered, "I don't think I will." She couldn't face a Thanksgiving service alone.

Dennis came to the kitchen doorway. "It just doesn't seem like Thanksgiving without Dad an Granny," he said in a forlorn voice.

Nora stood still in front of the stove. As she pushed her sandy-gray hair away from her forehead her voice was crisp. "You make Thanksgiving with what you have, Dennis O'Shea. Bob would have come home if he could."

Torrey helped Biddy set the table, her face thoughtful. Was Mom trying to make Thanksgiving with what she had, when Torrey hadn't come when she could?

From her window, the week after Thanksgiving

Torrey watched the plow turn under the stubble of the seminary field. She watched a tractor pull the harrow over the clouds until the golden field was dark brown. Then a seeder was driven around and around under the oaks.

It made Torrey feel more homesick than ever. The harvests were at home. The grapes had been picked and dried on the paper trays. The figs were long since shipped away to the packers. The olives had been milked from the limbs by the Filipino families, sorted and boxed and shipped to the cannery.

Mom would be up to her elbows in Christmas candies, and the home-cured olives would be soaking in the crocks. Soon Mom would be making the pecan pralines for the Christmas stockings.

Torrey turned from the window half blinded with tears. She had shared Thanksgiving well enough with Nora and Kate and the children. But Christmas?

Torrey took some of her precious chest money to buy Christmas presents. She found a record for Dave's new hi-fi, and a fancy screw driver because he liked gadgets. She borrowed Nora's sewing machine and made her mother some pillow cases with clover blossoms sprinkled all over them. Because she was afraid Mom might pop them right into the hope chest, she got a soft scarf just the color of Mom's eyes.

She found nice gifts for Nora and Kate, toys for the children, and an inexpensive glitter bag to go with Biddy's new formal.

But she couldn't find anything that seemed right for Dad. He didn't smoke. The kind of clothes he used were beyond her slender purse. She finally

195

spent more than she could afford on a book about Africa.

She didn't have the heart to write jingles to go with her gifts, as she always did at home.

She sent a box off to Cleve full of silly surprises, with a roll of film for his movie camera and a snapshot that Dave had taken of her at the beach, in a tooled leather frame. She wrote across the back, "With all my love—all of it—Muddy Face."

Then suddenly Christmas preparations were finished. The only thing left was learning Christmas stories for her two story hours. She worked hard on them. She learned "Schnitzle, Schnotzle, and Schnootzle" from Ruth Sawyer's *The Long Christmas*, a Mexican Christmas legend, and a story about the Hannukah lights. She sang carols with the children.

She enlisted Biddy's help and wrote a simple Christmas play for the cerebral-palsied children geared to their inability to get about. It somehow caught the spirit of Christmas, and the children painted the scenery and built a crude manger. Torey was surprised and delighted at the way they acted out the simple lines.

She tried to make her stories hold for the children the joy and wonder of Christmas, even if her own heart was heavy with the dread of it. She remembered what Roger in Elizabeth Gray's *Adam of the Road* had told his son: "A minstrel sings what his listeners want to hear. It's not for him to ease his own sorrows or to tell his own joys."

In Dr. Jordan's class everyone was learning and telling Christmas stories under the neat little mastern eye.

196

Torrey had warned them that he didn't like sentimental stories. So the tales they told were strong
and vibrant or delicate and poignant, according to
the taste of the teller. More than once she felt the
quick tears behind her eyelids. Christmas could be
a soul-wrenching business.

She worked in a sort of treadmill. This Christmas
was a chore to be toughed through. There was no
anticipation, no pleasure in any of it. Attack so
many things, get them done, check them off. She
shut her mind to the day that was coming with
leaps and bounds.

Dave had written, "Please, Torrey, Christmas will
be even worse than Thanksgiving. Bow your proud
neck, gal, and *come home!*"

Torrey didn't answer.

Then Nora had a letter from Bob. It came by
special delivery and arrived the week before Christmas. Torrey was in the living room when Nora
signed for it. She and Biddy watched while Nora
tore open the envelope with hands that trembled. A
slip of gray paper fluttered to the floor. It landed at
Torrey's feet and when she stooped to pick it up
she saw it was a check.

Nora turned white and then red, and white again.
She sat down on the davenport, staring at the letter
with unbelieving eyes.

"Mom! What is it?"

"God be praised!" whispered Nora. "Bob's sold
his book. It's a big advance he's had. He wants us
all to come, Kate and all of us. For Christmas. He's
sent us the money." She flung an apron over her
head and rocked back and forth.

Biddy began to spin on her toes. "Glory be! Mexico for Christmas. It's the thrill of a lifetime."

"And we're just the loons to be doing it too," cried Nora, wiping her eyes and wadding up her apron. "We'll fly, the whole of us, family rates. Where's the phone book? See about the reservations, Biddy, while I send him a telegram. Kate's got the whole week and more, and I've some time coming. And Torrey'll be going home yourself, of course."

"Of course," said Torrey through stiff lips as she slipped out the door and walked over to her own room.

She mailed her box home that evening. As she climbed the hill back to her room, she was thinking that it was all right for Nora to get a check from Bob, to pick up a whole family and fly to a foreign land. But it wasn't right for Torrey Thorne. Nora was married to Bob, and that made it right. Torrey Thorne wasn't married to Cleve Macklin, and it seemed wrong. But was it? And why? Why did she feel it would have been wrong to take Cleve's money and fly down to Chile to marry him? If it was right for them to love each other, wasn't it right for them to be married?

Torrey didn't know. Was it false pride, fear of criticism? It was these and more. Some inner compulsion, an inborn feeling that she must start her married life on a different basis. For Torrey Thorne her decision was, if not surely right, at least inevitable.

After the boxers had been taken to the vets, and the Siamese cat to a neighbor, Torrey drove Nora and Kate and the excited family to the airport, packed in like matches in Mona's car. She returned to a lonely, empty house.

"Going home for Christmas?" asked Clarissa at the library.

"No, I'm not." Torrey felt numb. This Christmas was something that mustn't come. To be alone was unthinkable. Going home was impossible. She wished she could hole in somewhere, like a bear or a chipmunk, and sleep through it.

The library Christmas party came and went. It was a potluck dinner, with the library tables groaning with food. There were nice presents with gay verses, and funny ones with still gayer rhymes.

On Friday only a skeleton crew was kept on. Torrey was slowly clearing up her desk, putting things away with great care, when Mona came out of Warren Brock's office, her face set.

Mona stopped when she saw Torrey still there. "I'm saying good-bye, Tor," she said in a brittle voice.

"Merry Christmas to you too, Mona."

"It's more than that. It's good-bye. I've just told Mr. Brock. I've quarreled with my whole family. So they're sending me off. I haven't got any fight left. Tell Clarissa for me, will you? I won't be at the library any more."

"Mona!"

"It's a fact. I just handed in my resignation. I'm taking the easy way out. I'm leaving."

"Where are you going?"

"South America. I leave for Santiago bag and baggage the day after Christmas with Cluney Mary Clevinger."

Warren Brock came to the door of his office, but Mona had pushed the outer door open, banged it behind her, and was gone.

Torrey walked home in a daze. Spinning through her head were things like, "I'm going after what I want," "Would you rather he wrote you for that freedom—and the ring?"

Miss Cluney Mary was taking Mona to Santiago. Torrey looked at that fact from all sides, and the taste of it was bitter. Because Mona didn't know that Clevinger Macklin was Torrey Thorne's man, but Miss Cluney Mary Clevinger did.

As she walked into Nora's yard, Torrey was surprised to see a black-clad priest sitting in one of the battered patio chairs. He was an elderly man. Beside him, flat on the iron table, was a sheet of window glass. On the glass was a miniature manger scene in soft putty. There was the Infant Jesus in swaddling clothes, in a troughlike manger. Beside the crib knelt a humble Joseph, some shepherds, a villager with upraised arms. There were an ox, donkey, and three kneeling sheep. Two fat little angels, one with a trumpet, another with cymbals, stood just beyond the crèche, and the priest was molding more putty in his slender fingers.

He rose as Torrey came in and, still molding the putty, bowed to her. "I am Father Vincent from the seminary," he said. "My boys were a little too lively this afternoon. One of them knocked a golf ball through your window. I didn't want you to come home to a roomful of shattered glass. And besides," his eyes twinkled, "I needed to retrieve the golf ball."

"You have made something very lovely in the meantime," said Torrey, examining with delight the manger scene on the sheet of glass.

He laughed, a little embarrassed. "Just puttering, as it were. I climbed the fence and measured the window. With your permission, I should like to replace the glass."

He smoothed and molded the small bit of putty in his hands into a shape, and pressed it down on the glass beside the others. With a gentle push it became the gracious, kneeling figure of the Virgin. "There," he said with satisfaction, "it is complete."

"It's lovely," said Torrey. "Can't you leave it?"

"You would be cold and wintry without a window glass, and the putty is needed to hold it in place." He pressed the large lump of putty down upon the figures. "Will it be a pleasant thing to think that you have the Holy Family as a frame for your outlook on life?"

"Do you ever make figures like that, Father Vincent? You have great skill."

"Yes. I make them. And they are sold at Christmastime. Most of them are made and painted. Only a few of the finer ones are fired."

"Are they very expensive?"

"Not the unfired clay figures. The money goes into our Chapel Fund."

Torrey wanted to ask for a set of them. She pulled herself up short. Her own funds were too low.

"You are here alone?" he asked. "With Nora Corrigan gone, you will be going home for Christmas?"

Torrey looked down at her hands. When she looked up again her eyes were filled with tears. "No, Father Vincent."

"Tsk! Tsk! Tsk! Is home so far away then?" He put the putty back in its greasy paper and picked up the pane of glass.

"No—I—that is—"

He walked over to the garage. With practiced fingers he pulled out the glass fragments and chipped away the old dried putty with his putty knife. "Be careful as you pick up the glass inside," he warned.

Torrey found the golf ball and brought it out. She watched Father Vincent as he deftly fitted the glass into the frame, applied the putty, beveled it, and smoothed it with his putty knife.

"There," he said. "You can keep an eye on us again, as soon as you clean the marks of the putty off the glass."

"Thank you," said Torrey. "I'll tell Nora what a fine new window she has. She'll be back after New Year's."

"A grand trip she'll have." He turned a stern eye upon Torrey. "Now. What's this about your not going home?"

"I—" Torrey stopped short.

"Where is your home?"

"Near Stockton, in the San Joaquin Valley."

"About two hours from here then."

"By car. But I'd have to go by bus and train, the long way around."

"You will have Saturday, Sunday, and Monday?"

"Yes."

"Then what sensible reason can you give me for not going home to spend Christmas where you belong?" He shot the question at her.

Torrey's voice was low. "I—I, well, I have quarreled with my father over the man I expect to marry. He—I have said I wouldn't go back until we could go together."

"Where is this young man?"

"In South America."

"And you may have to wait some time before you can be reconciled with your family?"

"Yes."

"And this is your idea of the spirit of Christmas?"

Torrey turned away in anger. What business was it of this strange priest to pry into her affairs? Because of a broken window, which was no fault of hers, he had chosen to set himself up as a judge of her actions, her decisions.

Father Vincent stood for a moment, watching her averted face. Then he sighed. "It is hard to be the one whose pride first gives way. But that is what Christmas is—the spirit of giving. I think you could give your family—all of them—no greater gift this Christmas than the supreme gift of yourself."

With a quick move he put his toes in the wire and was over the fence, walking across the springing grain in the field.

A little later that evening a younger priest knocked at her door. "Father Vincent sent this to you with his compliments," he said, handing her a small box. "These are some of his crèche figurines."

"How kind! How much do I owe him?" Torrey asked.

"Father said that he would like you to accept it as a gift."

When the young man was gone, Torrey opened the package. Inside were tiny, exquisite clay figures painted in soft blues and reds. With them was a card that said, "You can't run away from Christmas."

Torrey put the box on the table and reached for her jacket and the key to Nora's house.

Over the phone her voice was choked with tears. "It may take me all day tomorrow to get there, Dave, but I'm coming home."

"Take the train to the city, Torrey. I'll pick you up there in two hours." He must have turned from the phone. "What's that, Dad?" she heard him say. "Listen, Torrey, we'll all pick you up at the S.P. station in the city, as soon as we can make it. Mom and Dad are coming too."

Teach us delight in simple things,
And mirth that has no bitter springs

RUDYARD KIPLING—PUCK OF POOK'S HILL

21

CHRISTMAS WAS A GAY TIME for Torrey. There were no words between herself and her father. By mutual consent they had wiped their quarrel from the slate. Torrey had shut her mind to the day after Christmas when Mona would leave for Santiago.

"I saved the tree for you, Torrey," Mom said when they reached home. "I couldn't bear to trim it alone, and I couldn't get the men folk interested."

"We can all trim it, now Torrey's here," said Dad. But he sat in the big chair by the fire and watched them, his face relaxed, his eyes crinkled up with pleasure.

Torrey and Dave handled the old ornaments with tender fingers. The spun glass of some of the older ones was gray with age. The tiny golden cradle was tarnished brown. The tail of the little spotted rocking horse was gone. But the small trumpets still blew their thin, Christmassy notes; the little wooden spinning wheel still turned when the treadle was worked; and Hansel and Gretel waved diminutive arms at each other from opposite sides of the tree.

They clipped the candle holders to the branches and fastened the red and blue and green and yellow wax candles in them.

"It's getting harder to get these every year," complained Mom. "Guess I'll have to break down and get lights."

"Don't you dare!" said Dave and Torrey together.

When the tree was trimmed they sat down in front of the fire. The candles were lit. The lights were turned out. The pulsing glow of the candles set a thousand twinkling lights trembling from ornaments and tinsel and left dim, shifting shadows in the corners of the big room.

Mom picked up her well-worn Bible, leaving it open for a moment in her lap.

Torrey rested her head against the back of the davenport. It was as though she had never been away. This was the echo, the replica of all the Christmases since she was too small to remember. Candlelight and the Bible story. Mom and Dad and Dave, since Dave was so small he was held in the crook of Dad's arm as Mom found the place.

Would there ever be another? Would she be in South America for the next one? Could she make for herself, and for Cleve, and for their children this lovely, warm feeling of family unity? Would Cleve like this kind of a Christmas? He likes wind and sand and the sea, she thought. He'll like this.

With her book tilted to catch the light from the candles, Mom began the story, "'And it came to pass in those days . . .'"

They sang carols afterward. Then Mom brough

in a tall, foaming pitcher of hot chocolate and spicy Christmas cookies cut in the shapes of stars and bells, wreaths and holly. Just the smell of those cookies sent Torrey's mind back to the Christmas she had tried to stay awake all night to see Santa Claus, to her bicycle Christmas, to the year she got her first very own lipstick and silk stockings.

The next day Torrey unpacked her box to the family and wrote silly verses to go with her gifts.

Mom let her make the turkey stuffing. "No telling where you'll be for your first turkey. It always seems such an undertaking to a bride. But to my notion, it's the easiest meal there is to cook. Once the bird's stuffed, all you do is turn the heat low and time it. Christmas dinner is launched when the cranberry sauce is set."

Friends came down from the mountains with jugs of cider and a block of frozen quail and went away with boxes of Mom's pralines. A package arrived from Mexico marked "Open Before Christmas." In it were small, shining tin angels to hang on the Christmas tree. The gaudy card said, *"Salud!"* and was signed by Kate and Nora and Biddy, with kisses marked by Tim and Pat and Molly, and a grinning face drawn by Dennis.

On a small table, Torrey set up her tiny crèche, using a wooden salad dish that Dave sawed across for her as a background. The wood seemed just right and held a suggestion of a halo behind the manger scene.

She brought in from the garden an armload of greens and berries to hang, along with a string of tuna bells for the front knocker. Every time someone came there was the happy, brassy chime of bells.

The house was full of Christmas smells, spice and greens, baked cookies and fruit, and an indefinable something that was all of these and none of them.

On Christmas Eve Mom's brother David and three small grandsons came to spend the night with them. The mother of the boys was in the hospital with a new baby, but their father would be over early in the morning.

"Santa Claus brought us a girl," Uncle David was saying happily. "We told the doctor to send it back if he didn't. We're tired of boys in this family." He rumpled the hair of the nearest one.

"Her name is Torrey," said the youngest. "It's Torrey Elspeth Ames, and she weighs seven pounds, but I weighed eight."

Torrey felt a warm glow. Families were fun. She wondered about this little namesake, all seven pounds of small girlhood. She hoped she could see her before she had to go back.

More and more packages piled up beneath the tree. Stockings, ungainly red flannel affairs, limp with years of use, were hung on cup hooks from the mantel. When the excited little boys were safely off to bed, the grownups filled the stockings until they bulged with a candy cane, a horn, and a funny red-faced Santa peeking out of each top. Tricycles and a scooter appeared against the wall behind the tree.

At eleven that night all of the grownups but Uncle David, who chose to baby-sit, drove through the frosty countryside to church for the midnight service. When the choir of young people came down the aisle singing, "Oh come all ye faithful, joyful and triumphant," Torrey was thinking of the priest in the garden. If it hadn't been for him, she would have missed this. As Torrey bowed her head and the music swelled and the bells rang for the miracle of birth, she whispered thanks for the kindly, guiding hand that had sent her home for Christmas.

The little boys were awake even before it was light, blowing horns and shouting, "Merry Christmas, everybody! Come on, get up, it's Merry Christmas!"

"Just stockings before breakfast," said Uncle David, yawning mightily, his gray, rumpled hair standing on end above his pajama collar and bathrobe. But the boys were already riding furiously around the house on their tricycles and scooter.

Mom got the coffee started, and they went back to dress. They sat down to breakfast, nine of them now that the father of the brand-new little girl had come, to waffles, fiery brown quail, orange juice, milk, and coffee.

Then the packages were opened. It was fun to watch the children and their excitement over games and toys. New clothes were opened with a noticeable lack of enthusiasm, but the Davy Crockett moccasins were pounced upon with joy. "Anyway," said their father, "their pa and ma sure appreciate the clothes."

Torrey was delighted that her own gifts were mostly clothes, a new skirt and sweater, a smart raincoat. There were linens for the hope chest, and Mom gave her an impressive cookbook with mouthwatering pictures.

"Looks like an announcement," teased Uncle David.

Torrey grinned at him. "It does, doesn't it?"

"Do I know the lucky chap?"

Torrey glanced nervously at her father.

But Dad was rubbing his cheekbone. "We don't any of us know him," he said. "Like Torrey, we're waiting for him to get back from South America. Then we'll see that the whole family meets him."

The phone rang, and Dave went off to answer it. He hurried back, his face lit up like a jack-o'-lantern. "Long-distance call for Miss Torrey Thorne, from Santiago, Chile!" He looked after the flying figure of his sister. "Keep your feet on the ground, Sis," he yelled, "he'll wait."

"Cleve! Cleve! Is it really you? I've been so hungry for your voice!"

"Merry Christmas, Muddy Face!" Cleve could have been in the next room or across the street, his voice was so clear, so dear.

Had she opened his package?

"No, it must be still under the tree. Do you have mine?"

"Yes, and the best of it all is the message on the back of your picture. You sure, Torrey? Torrey, you *sure* you still love me?"

For goodness sake! Cleve was worried about *her*

"The minute you open my package, Torrey, you sit down and tell me if you like it. It's ours, just yours and mine. You'll have to pretend I'm there to put it on."

They talked until Torrey protested, "This is costing you a fortune, Cleve!"

210

"It's worth it. I had to hear your voice. I've had the call ordered ahead for weeks. I couldn't have faced Christmas without it."

When she came back from the telephone, her eyes like stars, all of Torrey's doubts had vanished. Let Cluney Mary and Mona go to South America. Let the long months drag by. Cleve Macklin was Torrey Thorne's man, body and soul.

A sudden thought struck her. If she had been stubborn enough to stay alone for Christmas at the little room in the garage, she would never have known this joy, this peace of mind on Christmas day. With the family gone from Nora's house, there would have been no one there to answer a long-distance call for Torrey Thorne from Santiago, Chile.

Torrey rooted around among the packages still under the tree until she found the box with the Chilean stamps. It wasn't very big. Inside the stout outer box was a smaller one with the name of a jeweler engraved on the top of it.

The whole family were watching her now, and Torrey was all thumbs. She pushed and pried and then pressed something. The lid of the tight little box sprang open. Inside, nestled in a bed of white velvet, was a ring with a star sapphire of heavenly blue, the milky star in its depths winking and blinking up at her. The little note said, "Because you're mine."

She took it out with trembling fingers. "It's my engagement ring," she said in a shaky voice. She slipped the lovely sapphire on her ring finger and held out her hand. "Cleve's and mine."

22

DAVE DROVE TORREY BACK. She was wearing the sapphire ring on a thin gold chain around her neck. There was, in her mind, a quiet relaxation. She could wait now, for Cleve, for their life together. She felt certain, sure of herself and of Cleve. She could put her whole heart into her work with the children, knowing the time would fly by.

She passed her courses at college with flying colors. There was a surprising A in Storytelling, a B in Children's Lit. With these units she would automatically get her degree in Library Science. She took a cake to the library to celebrate.

The next day Mr. Brock called her into his office. "I understand you are safely over the hump, Miss Thorne. Dr. Jordan gives you a high rating."

"I learned a lot from him."

"Our trustees approve of appointing you as full time Children's Librarian. Would you like that?"

"I'd love it. But I must be fair with you and wi

them. I'll be leaving the library to get married in a few months."

He threw up his hands. "First I lose Mona Kingsley, the best researcher we've ever had, and now you!"

"There'll be a whole new crop of graduates to choose from."

He shook his head. "Storytellers don't grow on trees or come with degrees. They are like really good teachers. Hertha Boatwright has been taking time off to listen to your stories. She would like to learn to tell them. Would you be willing to give her some training if you work full time?"

"I'd be glad to."

"Does anyone else know this news of yours or is it *sub rosa*?"

"Clarissa knows. No one else. I think I'd like to wait a little longer."

He nodded. "We can use you at full time for as long as you can stay. If the story hours can go on, I won't be so bitter about losing you."

Torrey plunged into the full-time job with enthusiasm. She told stories and gave talks and held classes in the library. She helped Hertha Boatwright learn stories and had her tell one story at each of the story hours. Torrey had her hands and her time full.

She often ate dinner with Nora and the children, bringing along fresh cooked crab or small, crisp artichokes from Half Moon Bay.

"It's good for Biddy to have you here, Torrey," Nora told her. "She thinks I'm an old dodo at the moment, but she'll listen to you."

One evening, when they had eaten all the crab they could crack out of the shells, Nora said, "Do the dishes, Biddy, while I get the children down," and added as Torrey started out with the platter of shells, "and don't just stand around, Biddy O'Shea, while Torrey does them!" But there was laughter in her voice as she shooed the three little ones ahead of her down the hall. There was a spring to Nora's step, a lilt to her voice.

"Nora's a new person since she came back from Mexico," said Torrey.

"Bob's coming home, that's why. Isn't it amazing what a man can do for a person?"

"If it's the right man." Torrey dumped washing powder into the sink and pushed a dish towel into Biddy's hand. She was thinking of Cleve.

"I wish Dave weren't so far off." Biddy sighed. "I'll be waiting years."

"If he's the right man," said Torrey with conviction, "it's worth it."

The next day she and Clarissa had a card apiece from Mona. Santiago was interesting. Fun. Nice people. Mona was flying to Brazil—might as well see the country while I'm here—but she was counting the weeks until she'd be home again.

Torrey was thinking as she cleared her desk one evening, I'll miss the library and Clarissa and Nora's family. If I had married Cleve last June, I would never have known the joy of telling stories in a story hour, of finding a new story just right for my kind of telling. I'd have missed the training under Dr. Jordan. I've learned poise, and how to face an audience, and the importance of the right word. No

214

matter what happens to Cleve and me in the years ahead, I can always fall back on this.

Late in April Torrey had a cablegram from Mona: *"Arriving San Francisco Airport five Wednesday flight 246 from Los Angeles. Bring my car meet me no argument. Mona."*

Torrey went in to speak to Mr. Brock. "Would you mind if I left early on Wednesday to meet Mona at the airport? She'll need her car. I'll make the time up somehow."

He grinned at her. "Don't worry about the time. You've earned a thousand hours with all this story preparation. I'll be glad to see Mona Kingsley back. I hope we can persuade her to go on with her work here."

Torrey was anxious to see Mona and to learn at first hand about Cleve and Santiago and Miss Cluney Mary—especially about Miss Cluney Mary. Cleve's letters had said over and over that no one could interfere again between Torrey and himself. But it was easier to say things in letters than to face up to a person like Cluney Mary Clevinger.

Torrey put on the French blue skirt and the matching sweater Mom had given her for Christmas. She slipped the blue sapphire ring off the chain and put it on her finger. The weather looked overcast enough to wear her navy and white checked raincoat with its jaunty cap, but not so stormy, she decided, that she needed to cover her best navy shoes with galoshes.

"Do I look all right?" she asked Biddy at noon.

"Real dark green," answered Biddy.

Clarissa said, "You look much too nice to be just meeting Mona!"

Torrey drove to the airport in plenty of time. She sat in front of the big window overlooking the concourse, watching the big planes circle and land and taxi in. She wished she were waiting to take one of them off to Santiago. She wondered if that time would ever come.

"Flight Number 246 from Los Angeles, Gate Number Four."

Torrey walked down the long hall. A handsome couple turned the corner, headed her way. Torrey was interested in the cut of the short karakul cape and the fur pillbox on the girl.

It was Mona, her face alight with laughter. Striding along beside her was Cleve Macklin.

"Torrey!" shouted Cleve.

In another few seconds Torrey was in his arms. Then he caught her face between his hands. His kiss was quick and hard and formal in the crowded hall, but his brown hands held her with a fierce intensity before he let her go.

Torrey was suddenly shy. Cleve was taller than she had remembered. When his gray eyes looked down at her, she felt the impact of it clear to her toes.

"Surprised?" asked Mona, laughing.

"Knocked silly!"

"Let's get a cup of coffee."

When they sat at a table in the dining room, Torrey found it hard to look at Cleve. She could feel the color coming and going in her cheeks. She found it hard to breathe evenly. She felt a terrible reluctance about letting her feelings show in her face. She yearned to reach out and touch Cleve's hand, to make sure he was really there. But she didn't dare. Her feelings might spill over and out of control, for Mona, for the whole world to see. She rolled her love for Cleve into a tight ball inside of her and tucked it away. She felt that he was making an effort to do the same. Nobody but Cleve must know how she felt.

"Now!" She laughed at both of them. "Tell me all."

"Let me see your ring first." Mona reached over and lifted Torrey's hand. "Torrey! It's beautiful!"

"Like it?" Cleve asked.

"Love it," she answered, very much as she had almost a year ago. But she didn't say, as she did then, something flippant about Gibraltar. "I dearly love it," she said quietly and laid the blue stone with its shining star against her cheek.

"We left Cluney Mary happily bossing the d'Alvarez family," said Mona, "when we decided to come home and surprise you. When she gets back she's going to talk Nora Corrigan into letting her send Biddy O'Shea to Notre Dame. Somebody told her Biddy had talent."

"I did," said Torrey.

"Think Biddy can stand up to Cluney Mary?"

"I think Biddy could stand up to St. Patrick."

Mona looked up at the white-clad waiter. "Three coffees. Black, Cleve? You always used to." She turned to Torrey. "When Cleve told me who his girl was, I nearly threw a fit. Why didn't you tell me?"

"I thought maybe you two—" began Torrey in a small voice.

Mona's hearty laugh rang out. "You and my mother and Cluney Mary! Nobody else, including Cleve and me, ever had the slightest notion—"

"I wouldn't say that!" drawled Cleve.

"Oh! Go on. We've known each other ever since we were born, Tor. He's a swell guy. But he's never been really in love with anybody on earth but Torrey Thorne."

Cleve grinned.

When they had finished their coffee, they drove back to Marysdale.

"Drop me off at the library, you two," said Mona. "I think Brock'll be there. I want to ask him for my job back, so I can spring it on the family when I get home. You take the car and go off some place and hold hands. Clarissa will drive me home."

After they had left Mona at the library, Cleve drove up the road past Nora's and up beyond the Clevinger house until they came to a high knoll with several oak trees. Cleve drove the car along some faint ruts between the trees and parked. They looked down over the green slopes to the sprawling cities below. Across the bay the Contra Costa Hills rolled in purple folds.

"I asked Gang if we could have this knoll to build our house when we come back next year."

"It's breath-taking!"

"I used to come here when I was a little boy, on a pony named Peanuts. When things got too thick for me at Gang's, I'd ride up here and pretend I was Kit Carson or Daniel Boone. I never had anyone to

218

play with. Once I built a playhouse in that big oak over there. You can still see the boards."

For the first time Torrey could see Cleve as a little boy, a lonely little boy. I'll make it up to him, she was thinking, all my life I'll make it up to him. "Did Miss Cluney Mary care, Cleve? About me, I mean?"

"Not after Mona and I got through with her. As soon as Mona found out it was you, they had a knock-down, drag-out. Mona told Gang the trouble with her was she didn't know quality when she saw it. She said to her, 'All you've ever had in your life is money. You've wrapped it around yourself like an armadillo all curled up in a hard, rigid shell.'"

"Oh, Cleve. Poor thing! What did she say?"

"Gang was speechless. Mona went right on. She said, 'You've dragged me down here, expecting me to cut that girl out, when Cleve and I settled that for ourselves, years ago.'"

"Did you, Cleve?"

"Settle it? Yes. Mona and I knew we weren't right for each other, in spite of all the family pressure. But I like her a lot."

"So do I. Even when I thought she was in love with you, and maybe you had been with her, I couldn't help liking Mona. But, Cleve, I don't want Miss Cluney Mary to feel that I'm taking you away from her."

"I don't think she does. When Mona got through, Gang looked so battered I just took her in my arms and told her you and I both would love her. Do you think you can?"

Torrey thought back over the times she had seen Miss Cluney Mary and of how unhappy she had been. It would take both of them to work it out. "I can try, Cleve."

"That's good enough. I told her we wanted this knoll to build a house big enough to raise a family and close enough so she could have them underfoot. That did it."

Torrey nodded. Maybe then she will learn to like me a little, she thought. "How long can you stay up here, Cleve? When do you have to go back to Santiago?"

"When we can go back together. I've promised Señor d'Alvarez I'd finish up what I started down there. I'll be doing some work in San Francisco for him while I'm here, to save him a trip up. He's anxious for me to bring you back. The whole family wants to meet you."

"Are you sure they'll like me?" Torrey felt a little uncertain.

Cleve laughed. "Certain sure. And I'll stay long enough to straighten things out with your dad. We'll give him a chance to see how much we care for each other." He put an arm across her shoulder and drew her cap off. His arm felt strong and warm and infinitely tender. He laid his cheek against her soft, dark hair. Still looking down over the slopes of the old Clevinger estate, he asked her, "Will you marry me then, Torrey Thorne?"

She looked down at the star glimmering in the blue stone on her finger. "Yes," she said. There was no room in Torrey's heart for any further doubts about herself and Cleve or their life together.